"Hoping to catch more compliments?" Pete laughed softly.

Jane walked toward him just as calmly as she had walked away a couple hours ago. Both times, though, her heart beat erratically. This time, her pulse raced, too.

"Maybe. Have I brought the right bait?"

"Maybe. Let's try it and see." He ran his hand up her arm, then to her shoulder. With one finger, he stroked the skin left exposed at the neckline of her dress, setting off ripples of pleasure everywhere he touched. "Smooth," he murmured.

He palmed the side of her neck, his long fingers tunneling into her hair. "Soft," he said.

"Is this Twenty Compliments now, instead of Twenty Questions?"

"Maybe."

He brushed his thumb across her lips. "Sweet," he said as he smiled.

Sliding his hands down to the small of her back, he pulled her toward him. "Sexy," he whispered.

"Is that another compliment for me," she murmured, "or a commentary on your technique?"

He tilted her chin up. Smiling, he shrugged.

"I'll let you be the judge of that."

Dear Reader,

I've been a hopeless romantic since grade school. From the first time I accompanied Nancy Drew and Ned Nickerson on a mysterious case to my first sighting of Rhett Butler and Scarlett O'Hara dancing around each other, I've wanted the hero and heroine of every story I read to end up together.

There's nothing like seeing a hero and heroine find their certain someone. And, of course, there's nothing better than watching that couple deal with their conflicts to reach their happy-ever-after. Usually, they manage to work things out on their own. But sometimes—whether they realize it or not—they need a little help.

In the small town of Cowboy Creek, New Mexico, that assistance comes from the local hotel owner, a meddling grandpa who wants to see all his granddaughters married and settled down. When Jed Garland turns his attentions to his loner ranch manager and his most stubborn granddaughter, he finds himself in for a real challenge!

I hope you enjoy your visit to Cowboy Creek. As always, I would love to hear from you. You can reach me through my website, barbarawhitedaille.com, or mailing address, PO Box 504 Gilbert, AZ 85299. You can also find me on Facebook, facebook.com/barbarawhitedaille, and Twitter @BarbaraWDaille.

All my best to you.

Until we meet again,

Barbara White Daille

A RANCHER OF HER OWN

BARBARA WHITE DAILLE

ISBN-13: 978-0-373-75577-6

A Rancher of Her Own

This edition published by arrangement with Harlequin Books S.A.

For questions and comments about the quality of this book, please contact us at CustomerService@Harlequin.com.

Printed in U.S.A.

Barbara White Daille lives with her husband in the sunny Southwest, where they don't mind the lizards in their front yard but could do without the scorpions in the bathroom.

A writer from the age of nine and a novelist since eighth grade, Barbara is now an award-winning author with a number of novels to her credit.

When she was very young, Barbara learned from her mom about the storytelling magic in books—and she's been hooked ever since. She hopes you will enjoy reading her books and will find your own magic in them!

She'd also love to have you drop by and visit with her at her website, barbarawhitedaille.com.

Books by Barbara White Daille

Harlequin American Romance

The Sheriff's Son
Court Me, Cowboy
Family Matters
A Rancher's Pride
The Rodeo Man's Daughter
Honorable Rancher
Rancher at Risk

The Hitching Post Hotel

The Cowboy's Little Surprise

Texas Rodeo Barons

The Texan's Little Secret

Visit the Author Profile page
at Harlequin.com for more titles.

To all the hopeless romantics in the world:
thanks for allowing me into the club.

And as always, to Rich.

Prologue

"About time we had a wedding around here, Paz." Jedediah Garland, proprietor of the Hitching Post Hotel on Garland Ranch, sat back in his chair in the establishment's large kitchen and smiled.

The hotel cook and Jed's longtime friend stood beside a counter with a slew of baking utensils spread out in front of her. "Do you think the banquet hall will be ready in time?"

"If the bride has her say about it, it will." That bride was the granddaughter he and Paz had in common, who was set to get married in the hall before the month ended. She was also in charge of the renovations going on all around the hotel.

He sipped from his coffee mug and thumbed through a selection of before-and-during photos of the reception hall. His wife had always been in charge of the weddings held at the Hitching Post, a part of the business he'd let slide for far too long. "My Mary must be looking down and smiling at us all."

Paz turned from her work to smile at him, too. "I'm sure she is. It will be nice to have a big wedding to prepare for again. We have you to thank for that, Jed."

"Well..." He shrugged, but there was no point in being modest around Paz. She had known what he'd done, every step of the way, to get their granddaughter and the cowboy she loved together. "I did have a hand in things, didn't I? And it wasn't easy. But you know, when the big day comes, I doubt we'll be needing a shotgun to get them down the aisle."

She laughed. "I would say you're right about that."

He reached for his coffee mug again.

At seventy-something and still going strong, he had a lot of living ahead of him and some dreams yet to be fulfilled. Seeing his business built up again was only one of those dreams. The other, he'd shared with no one but Paz.

He wanted family around him, which meant he intended to see all three of his granddaughters married and giving him additional great-grandkids as soon as possible.

Thankfully, he'd had smarts and luck enough to get the first bride- and groom-to-be to come to their senses. Eventually.

For the next couple, he would need to bring out the big guns.

Chapter One

Two weeks later

Some days started off right, then took a wrong turn. The minute Pete Brannigan walked into his ranch-house kitchen, he discovered this would be one of those days.

"Daddy!" his five-year-old daughter, Rachel, exclaimed. "Can Mama come to my graduation?"

His nanny and housekeeper, Sharon D'Angelo, turned from inspecting the contents of the refrigerator. The brief glance he exchanged with her held an entire conversation. They both knew the question wasn't *could* his ex-wife fly home for this milestone in her daughter's life, but *would* she?

"Good morning to you, sweetheart." He ruffled Rachel's wavy blond hair—so like her mama's—and reached over to the high chair to chuck his two-year-old son, Eric, under the chin. "And you, too, little man."

Eric gurgled something and handed him a soggy piece of cereal.

"Do you think Mama will come to see my graduation, Daddy?" Rachel asked.

He took his seat at the kitchen table beside her and said carefully, "I'm sure if she's not working the day you graduate, she'll be here." Not an outright fib. He would never lie to his kids or to anyone. Anyway, who knew what his ex-wife would do. Marina *might* take time from her jet-setting, fashion-model career to think of the kids she'd left behind. Although, as history had already shown, it didn't seem likely.

"Miss Loring said we get our invitations today. I'm inviting you and Mama and Eric and Sharon." She counted off on her fingers. "And Tina and Robbie and Paz." Tina was one of his boss's granddaughters. Robbie and Paz were Tina's son and grandmother. "And Bingo, too."

Smiling, he shook his head. "I don't think they'll let ponies into the school auditorium."

"Why?"

"They won't fit in the chairs."

"Oh. Well, I'll show Bingo the pictures later."

When Sharon held up the coffeepot, he nodded his thanks. He had long ago had a solitary breakfast here in the kitchen while she and his children still slept. As manager of Garland Ranch, he started work at an early hour, but as often as he could, he made it his business to get back to the house to see his daughter before she left for school.

"What about Grandpa Jed?" he asked Rachel.

"Of course Grandpa Jed," she said, rolling her eyes as if Jed Garland's presence at her graduation was a given. And it would be. "He wants to come, too, right?"

"Sweetheart, he wouldn't miss it."

Jed had always treated Rachel and Eric as if they were his own grandkids. Heck, from the time Pete had come to work as a wrangler here on the ranch, fresh out of high school, the old man had treated him like one of the family.

A couple of years ago, when Marina had taken off to seek fame and fortune, she'd left him to raise a three-year-old and a newborn alone. Jed had promptly promoted him into the vacant ranch manager's position, which included the manager's quarters, and increased his salary enough that he could comfortably pay for a live-in nanny to help take care of his kids.

"I have to save one for Grandpa Mark, too," she said.

Jed had always treated him better than his own father ever had. Now, though the man remembered the kids at birthdays and Christmas, his busy schedule kept him from visiting frequently. Rachel was aware of this, which was probably why she had given Jed top billing.

"And can I invite Jane and Andi to come, too?" A couple more of Jed's granddaughters. "And Missy and Trey?" Andi's two kids.

"I think they might all have gone home by the day of your graduation," he said.

She gasped. "They're coming for the wedding, right?"

"Definitely."

Jed's youngest granddaughter, Tina, was getting married later in the month. As flower girl, Rachel was even more wrapped up in the wedding than she was in her own special event. Along with her new fascination with floor-length dresses and three-tiered cakes, it looked as though she'd embraced the idea of extensive guest lists.

"Well," she said, "then they *have* to come to my graduation, too."

Better to try to let her down easy, something he'd had plenty of practice doing, thanks to Marina. "There are other kids in your class, you know, and they have friends and family to invite. I'm not sure your teacher plans to give you that many invitations."

"I'll tell Miss Loring she *has* to. I can't leave anybody out. Like Tina and the wedding."

"Well, we'll see." Personally, he'd just as soon have Tina and her fiancé, Cole, one of his wranglers, leave *his* name off their list. Pointless to hope for that, though, when they had already roped him into becoming a member of the wedding party.

After a look at the kitchen clock, he leaned over to kiss Rachel's forehead. "I'll see you after school. It's time for you to go and brush your teeth."

"*And* get my backpack. To bring all my invitations home." She slid from her seat.

As she left the room, he and his housekeeper exchanged another glance. "The bossiness hasn't let up any, has it?" he asked.

The older woman smiled, adding a few more wrinkles to her lined face. "As I keep saying, she'll outgrow it."

"Yeah? Before or after one of the bigger kids at school thumps her on the nose for pushing him around?"

"She could probably talk herself out of a fight with anybody in that kindergarten class."

"It's the middle-schoolers I'm worried about."

Sharon laughed. "She'd handle them, too." She hesitated. "I'm not condoning her bossiness, Pete. I've tried talking with the child, and she can almost talk rings around *me*. It's given me a whole new crop of gray hair."

He didn't know what he'd do without Sharon, a widow who had become his nanny and housekeeper shortly after he and the kids had moved into the house. She had given up her small apartment in Cowboy Creek and relocated to the ranch full-time. She was a grandmother herself, with several grandkids of her own, and her experience had saved him many times over the past couple of years. Now she sounded worried, as if her job depended on teaching his daughter social skills.

"Hey, that's not what I hired you for. And trust me, I've tried to talk with her, too. To get her to see she'll win more friends with honey than harassment. But you're right—she'll outgrow it. Sooner than later, I hope."

It was his turn to hesitate. Before too long, he needed to have another discussion with Rachel, and it would have to cover more than her social skills. He kept his gaze on Eric, who sat playing with the dry cereal on his high-chair tray. "I can't do anything about Jed's family staying around for the graduation."

"You can't do anything about Marina, either," Sharon said softly.

He sighed. "I know. But dammit, Sharon, she's disappointed the kids too many times already." And each time, he'd felt like punching something—not the best example to set for his talks with Rachel about her conduct. With every one of Marina's cancellations, he was forced to break the news to his daughter, and he couldn't deal with seeing her turn so quiet, so withdrawn, for days afterward.

Eric pushed a few pieces of his cereal over the side of the tray.

"Now, don't you start, little man. Your sister's enough of a handful right now." Pete caught both his son's wrists and pressed them together between his palms.

Familiar with the game, Eric laughed, slipped his hands free and pounded the tray, making the scattered cereal bounce. Pete reached down to pick up the pieces that landed on the floor.

"Leave that," Sharon said. "I'll sweep up when he's done."

"Thanks. You're the best." He dropped a few pieces of the cereal into the kitchen trash and then planted a kiss on Eric's blond curls. "I'd better head out. Charlie's due to stop in anytime now." Charlie, the local vet, was coming to take a look at one of the mares with a leg injury. "I'll see you all later."

He left the house and strode in the direction of the barn, which sat within easy walking distance, even for Rachel, who spent plenty of time in the adjacent corral and at the Hitching Post.

As he thought again of his daughter, he shook his head.

She had recently begun dramatizing every little incident—very much like her mother always had and still did on her rare visits to town. At the thought of the public scenes Marina had put him through in the past, he shuddered. He dreaded the idea of Rachel taking on more of her mama's traits. Already, her bossiness seemed like her way of controlling situations. Of getting extra attention.

Or maybe he read too much into his daughter's behavior. It was hard to tell. Sometimes he didn't know for sure how to read either of his kids. The thought made him heave another sigh. Though his position as manager of Garland Ranch routinely included long hours, rough riding, unpleasant tasks and backbreaking chores, none of that came close to the challenge of being a single dad.

TRUE TO FORM, once Rachel's questions about her mama had sent Pete's morning off on its wrong turn, the rest of the day followed suit. Though he would never trade his job on the ranch for anything, by quitting time he felt ready for a few weeks of selling ice in Antarctica.

Looking beyond the mare he was tending to, he eyed his boss, who stood just outside the stable door.

Jed had recently made it his mission to revitalize the Hitching Post, the honeymoon hotel on the property, and had lined up all his granddaughters to help with the transformation. Twice in the space of as many minutes, the boss had brought up the name of one of those granddaughters. A name Pete was all too familiar with, belonging to a granddaughter he wanted to go nowhere near.

Plenty of times over the past few years, he'd seen Jane Garland—from a distance—on her visits to the ranch. She didn't much care for riding, but she would walk over with her cousin Andi when she rode, always resulting in more grief for him. Other than that, their paths had no need to cross, which suited him just fine.

But now he had a bad feeling about the direction of Jed's conversation.

"Almost done, girl," he murmured to Starlight. He kept his focus on her sore foreleg as he applied the ointment the vet had dropped off that morning.

"Won't be long," Jed went on, "before we'll have the place on the map."

The boss had gotten all fired up about increasing business for the hotel. Pete couldn't find any fault with the plan. Although managing a spread the size of Jed's already provided him with more than full-time employment, he wouldn't balk at the extra work. He'd always just added the dude-ranch activities onto his list of responsibilities.

"Andi will fly in with her kids by the end of the week. But Jane—" *third mention* "—decided to come a couple of days ahead. She'll be taking pictures at the wedding rehearsal, you know."

He nodded, his focus still on Starlight. "Yeah, Cole said." Cole had told him that news and a lot more about all of the boss's granddaughters.

Since his divorce, happy matrimony was the last thing he wanted to think about. But Jed and Cole both made sure to keep him up-to-date on all the wedding plans.

He couldn't blame either of the men. After all, he *had* agreed to be one of the ushers, which meant attending that danged rehearsal. And the wedding, of course.

"Starlight's leg is looking good," he told Jed.

Finished with the mare's treatment, he went to the sink in one corner. The sound of running water kept Jed quiet for a moment, giving Pete a chance to think.

The boss had also kept him up-to-date on the renovations going on over at the hotel. That made even more sense, as increased business there meant more dudes for his cowhands to work with and entertain on the ranch. For anything connected with the hotel guests, he and Jed always coordinated with Tina.

"Jane," Jed went on, "wants to take some photos around the hotel. The rooms downstairs, some of the guest rooms that are already finished…for the new website."

"Sounds good." He grabbed the towel from beside the sink.

"I want you to give her a hand."

He froze with the towel halfway up one wet forearm. Water ran down the other arm and off his elbow. *Drip... drip...drip...* Like water torture. Like the sound of Jed's request echoing in his brain.

The boss's blue eyes looked guileless enough. But then, he couldn't know how much his manager wanted to avoid this granddaughter, for a whole list of reasons.

He'd had enough of the teenage Jane mouthing off to him during his early days working as a stable hand on the ranch. As a dyed-in-the-wool cowboy, he had no interest in being around a city slicker. And those stories Cole had told him recently only reinforced his determination to avoid her. Her drive for success and single-minded focus on her career gave her too much in common with his fashion-model ex-wife.

Pete finished drying off and hung up the towel again. "What does she need with a cowboy, if she's only taking a bunch of pictures?"

"She'll be setting things up, moving furniture around. I want someone to do the heavy lifting."

"I can spare one of the stable hands for that. They're fine about doing whatever jobs they're given, even ones not in their job description." He forced a laugh. "Since moving furniture's not in mine, either, I'm sure you don't want your foreman—"

"I *do* want my foreman on this job."

"Speaking of jobs, I'd better get going." *And get the heck out of here before I say something I shouldn't.* "There's a lot of territory to cover this morning." He crossed the barn to take a set of reins from their hook. "It's June, Jed. I don't need to tell you how busy that makes us around here."

"And I'll tell you this, flat-out straight the way I always do. I want someone I can trust to be alone with my granddaughter."

Eyebrows raised, Pete turned back. From the stories Cole had told him about Jane, a New Yorker who traveled all over the world for her job, he couldn't think of any woman more able to handle herself. Which meant…

"I'm not saying anything against the boys," Jed continued as if he'd read his manager's mind. "I trust every one of 'em. But there's no one I have more faith in than you."

"I appreciate the vote of confidence, boss." He swallowed hard. "But—"

"And as I recall," Jed interrupted heavily, "when it comes to job descriptions, the two of us don't much stick to formalities between us, do we?"

"No, we don't," he agreed, knowing those words had just sealed his fate.

He owed the boss for providing everything he needed to take care of his kids.

And now, all too plainly, the man had called in his debt.

Chapter Two

As a shadow fell across the open doorway of the barn, Pete took one look, lowered the pitchfork he was holding and set it against the wall outside the stall. Frowning, he stared at the woman who stepped into his domain.

Technically, he didn't own anything on the ranch. Still, even the thought of this particular granddaughter of Jed's coming near the barn left him feeling possessive. Old habits might die hard, but old memories never left you.

He'd heard from Cole that Jane had arrived at the Hitching Post the night before.

Feet planted wide, he rested his hands on his hips. "Can I help you?" He hoped not. In fact, since his conversation with Jed a couple of days ago, he'd kept his fingers crossed that the boss would change his mind about having him babysit Jane.

From a strap around her neck hung a camera that probably cost more than he spent in a year on clothing for him and the kids. Without answering, she raised the camera and aimed it at him, making him feel like a bug under a microscope. Before he could react, she had fired off a couple of shots.

He raised a brow. "I don't know what you think you're doing, but you can stop doing it right now."

"Just testing the lighting in case I want a few promo shots."

"You reckon newlyweds will care about the inside of a barn?"

"Atmosphere," she said shortly, turning to click off a series of photos down the length of the stalls.

Silently, he watched her. Over the years he'd avoided coming in contact with her, his long-distance eyesight must have begun to fail. He hadn't realized she looked this good close-up. Tall and slim, she had pale, perfect skin he wouldn't dare touch with his workman's hands and straight black hair that glistened in the light, tempting him to run his fingers through it.

Every time he'd seen her, she was dressed head to foot in black, and now was no exception. He didn't get why anyone would feel an attraction for the color, a stark reminder to him of funerals and the day they'd laid his mama to rest. But he managed to look beyond Jane's taste in clothes long enough to check her out.

Today she wore a pair of jeans topped by a loose T-shirt. The only color on her—if you could call it that—came from the cold strands of the silver necklace dangling almost to her waist. She looked as out of place in here as he'd have looked at an opera house.

When she focused on the final stall in the row, old Daffodil stuck her head through the open door. Swaybacked, bowlegged and cantankerous when she chose to go that route, the mare lived out her days in comfort thanks to Jed, with Pete's assistance.

Jane gave a throaty chuckle that yanked his attention back to her. The sound seemed to echo in the cavernous barn…and to rattle something deep inside him.

"C'mon, girl. Let's see the profile."

"That'll be the day when you can get *her* to pay attention," he said with a grin, trying to shake off his reaction to her.

"I pity the animals you work with, if that's your attitude toward them."

His grin slid away. "And what are you, a horse whisperer?"

"Maybe."

"Besides, it's not my attitude." He wondered why he was bothering to explain. "Daffodil's as high-spirited as they come, but danged stubborn, too." The words made a picture in his mind of a teenager giving him back talk. "Does that description remind you of anyone?"

She looked his way again. Even with her back to the sunlight in the doorway, he saw her eyes gleam.

She remembered that summer vacation she'd spent here on the ranch, all right—he'd bet the jar of Buffalo nickels he was saving for his son on that.

"You think you're going to win old Daffodil over to your side, huh?" he said.

"Yes. With the right incentive."

As she passed him on her way to the stall, the scents of vanilla and spice drifted toward him, light but noticeable enough to set off a craving for something sweet, and surprising enough to make him blink. She'd never seemed the sweet, vanilla type.

She held out a hand. "What do you say, Daff? Want to be a cover girl?"

At the question, Pete's shoulders went rigid.

The old mare dipped her head, as if giving Jane a royal nod and permission to do what she liked.

Dang, the woman has a way with a horse, after all.

Then he noticed she held her palm upward. "That's cheating."

"All's fair in love and getting the perfect shot." Once

Daffodil took the sugar cube from her hand, Jane stepped back and began clicking again.

"I doubt any newlyweds will want souvenir photos of an old, past-her-prime mare."

"These are for me."

He couldn't keep his eyebrows from shooting up in surprise. He couldn't keep from needling her, either, and blamed it on those bygone days when a teenager seven years his junior had made his life a misery. "Gonna put them up on the wall in your New York high-rise?"

"Who's gonna stop me?"

He narrowed his eyes. Then he noted the rueful twist of her lips. She was baiting him. The idea gave him a rush of pleasure he wasn't sure how to handle.

"So, you *do* recall all those times you gave me grief."

"I might have a faded memory or two," she admitted.

When she moved toward the door, he remained where he stood, watching her silhouette against the bright sunlight.

She turned. "Way back then," she said, "I was just a kid asserting my rights."

You're sure not a kid anymore. He brushed the thought away. "You were being a pain in my butt."

She grimaced. "That too, maybe. But you can't tell me you didn't deserve some of it, considering your new job had swelled your head to about the size of this barn door."

She rested her back against the frame. Her stance highlighted unsuspected curves beneath that loose, dark shirt, which instantly made his jeans tight below his belt.

Yeah, he'd called it right about her not being a kid.

He hoped she planned to go away soon—not just from the barn but, once the wedding was over, from the ranch and from Cowboy Creek. He couldn't blame that thought on memories of the past, his desire to get back to work or even the sight of her gazing regally down her nose at him the way Daffodil had looked at her.

No, he wanted her long gone because she'd turned out to be one fine-looking woman. Because she was making him want things he had no time in his life for now. And because she was *still* too many years younger than he was and would *always* be the boss's granddaughter.

Yeah—think of the boss. "That was my first full-time job," he told her. "I was trying to make an impression."

"Oh, you did that, all right. I'm glad you didn't say 'a *good* impression,' because you didn't come close to one. I don't like men—people—who think they can order others around. And you definitely had a case of that back then."

"I was in charge of the horses—"

"Under my grandpa's direction."

"—and watching out for them was part of my job."

"He's given you another job now, too, so he tells me."

"Yeah. Playing nursemaid."

"Thanks, old man," she shot back, "but I don't need that kind of help. An assistant is more like it. What's the matter? Is the job beneath you?" She shrugged. "If you don't like the idea, I won't have a problem getting someone else."

He'd bet she wouldn't. As long as she managed to keep that smart yet sexy mouth of hers shut, any of his boys would be happy to assist her. He wouldn't, but turning down Jed's order wasn't an option. "I didn't say anything against the idea. I've got no problem with moving furniture around."

"Good. Then I'll meet you in the lobby tomorrow morning at nine."

To his satisfaction, she didn't seem to be any happier about the assignment than he did.

IN THE HOTEL dining room the next morning, Jane joined in on the conversation about the upcoming wedding. The bride and groom made the most happy and genuinely loving couple she'd seen in a while.

She relaxed over a plateful of Paz's breakfast treats. Or at least, she tried to relax. That hadn't been an item on her agenda in a while. Working seven days a week kept her mind busy and her body active. Lately, having to sit still made her uneasy and all the more eager to be on the move.

Her meeting in the barn with Pete Brannigan had left her uneasy, too.

The cowboy didn't scare her. With those amazing hazel-green eyes and all those bulging muscles, he was too darned hot for any woman in her right mind to be frightened away. Still, there was something about him that pushed all her buttons. That had made her jump to a knee-jerk reaction every time he'd opened his mouth. That made her snap to attention…

Of course.

Years ago, she had seen how much he acted like her father, an Army general. Yesterday, Pete's take-charge attitude at their first meeting in years had strongly reinforced those memories, proving he hadn't changed a bit. But she would do her job—even if that meant working with the insufferable man.

"Don't forget, Jane—"

Startled, she returned her attention to Tina.

"—we've got to go up to Santa Fe to pick up our gowns. We might as well wait till Andi gets here, and then we can have our final fittings together."

Jane laughed. "In that case, I'd better stay away from Paz's apple tarts, or I won't get the zipper closed on my dress." She pushed the dessert platter a few inches away from her.

"Ally and I are the ones who should worry about that," Tina said, referring to her best friend and maid of honor. "You and Andi are so slim."

"*You* don't need to worry a bit," Cole said to his bride.

They smiled at each other as Cole casually draped his arm across Tina's shoulders.

A beautiful pre-wedding portrait.

But you're not on the job right this minute.

Despite the fierce reminder, she wished she hadn't left her camera on the far side of the dining room.

As if she'd heard the thought, Tina said, "I'm glad you'll be taking pictures at the rehearsal dinner. But the day of the wedding, you won't forget you're a member of the bridal party, will you?"

"Yeah," Cole said. "We've got a photographer lined up, so you'll have the day off."

"I don't know," she said, only half joking. "Sometimes it feels like those cameras are extensions of my hands. I don't go anywhere without them."

"Speaking of going somewhere…" He kissed Tina and rose from his seat. "I'd better hit the road, or I won't be back before lunch with the supply order."

"Say hi to Ally when you see her," Tina said. Her maid of honor worked at the hardware store in town.

Once Cole had left, Tina turned back to Jane. "Maybe we need to take those cameras away from you, so you'll behave yourself at the wedding," she teased.

"We can put them in my toy box," said Robbie.

Jane smiled at her cousin's four-year-old. "Your toy box?"

He nodded. "In my bedroom. Mama takes my toys away and puts them in the toy box."

"Oh, I see," she said, searching for something to add. Her work might require she spend her life around people, including children, but she reserved in-depth interviews only for adults. Either way, she didn't encourage her subjects to interact with her. She wanted to capture them in natural poses and real-life situations. Often all too real.

"Mama takes the toys when I don't listen," Robbie explained.

"Oh. Maybe I should not listen, once in a while, too, and then I won't work so much."

As if.

She looked up to find her grandfather eyeing her from the head of the long table. Suddenly, she realized some of her uncertainty came from her current "assignment."

"You and Pete going to get started this morning?" he asked.

"We are," she confirmed. "But not for a little while. I'm not rushing through Paz's great breakfast."

After the photo shoots she had just completed, with three European trips in the space of a month, she shouldn't plan to rush through anything this week. She deserved a break. Just not one that involved sitting still.

She loved her grandfather and felt more than happy to help with the hotel revamp. Taking a few photos here and setting up the ranch's new website would be a piece of cake compared to the Sarajevo shoot and other assignments she'd worked on.

She didn't mind spending a few extra days at the ranch, either, to get some of Grandpa's photos out of the way—even if the job came with the drawback of having Pete around.

He'd been right yesterday about the way she had acted years ago, about being a pain whenever she went near him.

Long before that summer, she'd already seen how girls'

hormones made them do silly, stupid things around boys, and she had determined never to be like those girls. As an Army brat who had attended a succession of schools overseas by the time she hit her teens, she hadn't ever met a boy she'd waste her time crushing on, let alone want to go out with.

Not, of course, that General Garland would ever have allowed his daughter to date at that age.

But the year she turned thirteen, on her summer vacation to Garland Ranch, she had run into Pete Brannigan outside the barn. Instantly, she understood why girls did silly, stupid things around boys. Besides, at twenty, Pete wasn't a boy but a man.

Unfortunately, only two minutes afterward she discovered he was a younger version of her father. Hormones or no hormones, that was the end of her interest.

It was her thirteenth year all over again yesterday, when her first glance at Pete had given her equally silly though much more grown-up thoughts. Yet their run-in and his crack about being her "nursemaid" proved he had only gotten worse over time. If he thought she would sit back and let him boss her around—the way he'd always done whenever she had come near the barn or corral with Andi—he was in for a big surprise.

TO PETE'S SURPRISE, after he and Jane met in the hotel lobby, they settled into a routine with her doing the directing and him doing the grunt work. Nothing very strenuous, as they'd started in the sitting room just off the lobby.

His job consisted of shifting tables, couches and chairs and putting them back into place. It involved very little talking and a whole lot of looking, which suited him fine.

"Midmorning will be a good time for us to get the

common areas done," Jane had said yesterday. "The guests will either be sightseeing or taking riding lessons out at the corral."

Exactly where he should have been, overseeing those lessons. Instead, he'd notified all the hands they could reach him on his cell phone if necessary.

The morning had passed much more quickly and with much less bickering than he had anticipated—probably because once Jane got behind the camera, she stayed there.

He stood leaning against the door frame, watching as she worked her way silently around the area.

"I don't see much of a difference," he said finally. "And the room always looks comfortable enough to me."

"It's a matter of perspective, especially with a static shot. Of finding the right balance between comfort and space." She continued moving, her gaze on the camera, the shutter clicking away. "For now, we're looking at still photos for the website and print promotion, but we might eventually shoot some panoramic video. Grandpa's going all out with his ideas for the revamp."

"I can't see anything wrong with the hotel the way it is."

"You don't like change, do you?"

"Not much."

"How do you feel about weddings?"

"I don't like them at all."

"Lovely." She glanced at him. "Then I'd guess you have no plans to be the life of the party at Tina and Cole's reception?"

"Not hardly."

"What are the chances you'll be able to hide your feelings?"

"I'll manage."

Camera lowered, she turned his way. "What happens when the bridal suites are refurbished and the hotel starts booking complete wedding parties?"

"Doesn't make a difference. The hotel guests are all the same to me, and we entertain the guests, period."

"You won't make much of a spokesperson for the Hitching Post."

"Good thing I'm not looking for the job, then, isn't it?"

She raised a dark eyebrow but didn't respond to that. Instead, she looked at her watch. "Why don't we stop in at the kitchen for something to drink."

Paz was bustling around the room, and Maria, one of the maids, was assisting her. This close to lunchtime, they were too busy to do much but give him a quick hello. He nodded in return while Jane poured a couple of glasses of iced tea and handed one to him.

They went through the kitchen door onto the back porch. Over at the corral, he could see the stable hand grooming one of the stallions.

He took a long swig of tea and leaned against the porch railing.

He could feel the noonday sun warming his back, spreading heat through him. Better to believe that than admit the truth, even to himself. Not that he had anything to be ashamed of with his reactions. Jane Garland wasn't his type. Her preference in clothing did nothing for him. He didn't care for her made-up face or her long nails, and her high-tech toys turned him off. But as he'd already acknowledged to himself, she was a good-looking woman—a *sexy*, good-looking woman—and standing this close to her would get any man overheated.

He gulped down another mouthful of cold, sweet tea.

"I'll give you a break till this afternoon," she said. "I

don't want you telling Grandpa I kept you so busy you couldn't do the job he pays you for."

"Excuse the pun, but you really focus on your work, don't you?"

"I try to."

"How'd you get to be such a perfectionist?"

She laughed. "You've met my father, haven't you?"

"Yeah, lots of times." He took another drink and wished he hadn't brought up the subject. Not if it was going to lead to a discussion about their parents.

He didn't like talking about his mother, who had passed on when he was in grade school. For other reasons, he avoided talking about his dad, the big-shot lawyer.

"Something wrong with the tea?"

The question made him realize he was scowling. "No, the tea's fine. What does your dad have to do with your perfectionism?"

She shrugged. At her movement, the necklace she wore shifted across the front of her blouse. Sunlight glinted off the silver links, drawing his attention to her curves. Again.

"He's an Army general," she said. "That ought to explain it." She downed her iced tea and licked the sweetness from her upper lip.

Almost without thinking, he did the same. Then he blinked and wiped his mouth with the back of his hand. It wasn't moisture he was attempting to brush away, but a sudden thought he had no business having.

"I'd better get inside and see if I can help Paz with anything. Are you done with that?"

He nodded and held the empty glass out to her. She moved to reach for it, then froze for a moment, her gaze locked with his. They stood so close, it wouldn't take but a half step to bring their bodies together. Before he could say yea or nay on giving that a try, she stepped back.

"We'll meet in the lobby again, around two?"

Her tone was cool as usual, but had her voice wobbled just a bit?

Glad to see her return to the house, he stayed there for a minute, leaning against the rail.

Maybe she'd been right to question his ability to hide his feelings. Which meant he'd better work twice as hard at keeping his thoughts—and his reactions—in line.

What *he* questioned was the flare of interest in her eyes…and the wisdom of testing if it was real or his imagination.

Chapter Three

Not long after the start of their afternoon session at the Hitching Post, Pete's memories of the smart-mouthed teen Jane had once been came rushing back full force. A very good thing, as it made him forget the crazy questions that had plagued him since they'd parted that morning.

She had gone all out with the rearrangement of one of the hotel suites "to catch the right slant of the sun," and her never-ending orders rubbed him the wrong way.

He set the stepladder she had requested next to the claw-foot tub in the suite's bathroom.

She ran plenty of hot water and added several squirts of a liquid soap into the flow, creating a cloud of fluffy white suds that rose well above the edges of the tub. The amount of bubbles would have satisfied even his daughter.

Arms crossed, he leaned against the door frame and watched Jane go up the ladder. "You do realize that sticker on the step you just breezed past says not to climb any higher, right?"

"I need to find the best angle." She sat astride the top of the ladder, one foot braced on the paint tray.

While he could and did admire the view, he didn't think much at all of her position. "I'll tell you what you'll find if you're not careful—your head cracked open after you fall into that tub."

"Not your problem."

"No. Not until I have to explain the situation to Jed."

"Don't worry—Grandpa won't sue you. And if you're that concerned, I'll sign a waiver." After a few clicks with her camera, she frowned and glanced toward the window near the head of the tub. "Can you move that curtain to one side?"

"It's bright as day in here already."

"The sun's going down, though, and I want to catch the light streaming in across the bubbles."

He'd called it right about her liking things just so. He flipped up the bottom of the curtain to loop it over the rod.

Again, she frowned. "Not exactly the effect I was looking for. As I said the first time, could you hold the curtain aside?"

"You really are a perfectionist, aren't you?"

For a moment, her lips pressed into a tight, straight line. Then she smiled. "You ought to see my hospital corners when I make a bed."

"Was that an offer?" The words slipped out of his mouth before he had a chance to think about the consequences. What was it about Jane that scrambled his brain?

She gave him a slow smile. "Cowboy, if I made you an offer, it would be *perfectionistically* clear."

The image that brought to mind left him breathless. He turned and shoved the fabric across the rod, then stood looking through the window. One way or another, he needed to forget these thoughts he was having about her. Or find out if he actually had seen that spark of interest earlier.

"You know, if you'd really rather not do this," she said mildly, "you could send someone else to take your place."

No, he couldn't, thanks to Jed.

Damn. He owed the boss so much, yet here he was, having inappropriate thoughts about the man's granddaughter.

He turned and looked up at her on the stepladder. "Just looking out for your safety."

"Thanks, but that's not necessary. I've been in much riskier places than on a ladder in a hotel room."

"Name two."

"At the scene of a government overthrow. And undercover in a drug lord's headquarters."

She'd made the statements so matter-of-factly, he couldn't question the truth of them. Her blank expression told him not to pursue this part of their conversation.

He'd heard Jed complain often enough about his granddaughter's job as a photojournalist. Till now, he'd had no idea of the level of danger involved. He suspected Jed didn't, either.

"And you've gone from that to this?"

She laughed, low and husky, setting off that rattling sensation inside him again. "When Grandpa speaks, I listen."

He thought of what she had said about her father, another topic she didn't seem inclined to discuss. "And when your dad speaks, you pay attention, too?"

"Something like that." She swung her leg over the top of the ladder and clambered down the steps, one hand held in front of her to protect the camera on its strap. "I think we're done here."

He glanced at the tub. "That's a waste of hot water. And not to mention all the fun we'd miss out on with the bubbles."

"Is it your turn to make me an offer?"

"Something like that." He hadn't deliberately echoed her words, but they were out before he could stop himself.

"You're right. Why waste all those bubbles? Why don't you feel free to jump in—" she raised the camera "—and give me a big smile."

He stepped forward, reaching out to cover the lens. It put him close enough to see the pure silver gray of her eyes surrounded by lashes as dark as her hair. "I'll pass on that offer, too."

"Why? Are you camera-shy?"

The real answer would take too long and tell her much more than he wanted her to know. "Let's make things perfectly clear, the way you like 'em." He tugged gently on her silver chain and watched her eyes darken. "Honey, I'm not shy about anything."

IGNORING PETE'S BOOTS clomping behind her, Jane walked down the hotel's stairs to the first floor on legs that weren't quite as steady as normal.

In the suite upstairs, his teasing hadn't meant a thing; it had just been his way of yanking her chain. Of trying to get the upper hand, the way he had always done—though years ago, he'd certainly never attempted that by moving in close enough for a kiss. To her shock, his nearness had made her pulse pick up. Now the idea of kissing him made it spike.

She needed to get a grip on more than her camera.

As they reached the lobby, Tina came out from her office behind the registration desk. "There you are. Pete, Rachel's in the dining room."

Jane noticed Pete shoot a glance toward her before looking back at Tina. "The kids are home already? I didn't realize it was that late."

"They were just dropped off a few minutes ago."

"I'll check in and say hello."

Before he could turn to go down the hallway to the dining room, they heard footsteps approaching from that direction. She hadn't seen Pete's daughter for quite a while, but she recognized the small, blond-haired girl dressed in a red T-shirt and denim shorts who entered the lobby, followed by Jed.

To her surprise, the girl gave her a big grin.

"Hi, Jane!" she shrieked. "I knew you would come back because you have to be in the wedding. And we have to try on our dresses. Mine's soooo pretty. Like your dress and Andi's and Ally's—well, but mine's smaller. Ally's is different because she's the best maid and—"

"Maid of honor," Pete put in.

"—maid of honor and she gets to be special. But I get to be special, too, because I'm going to carry flowers. Nobody else gets to carry flowers like mine—did you know that? And nobody else gets to drop them on the floor. Only me, right, Daddy?"

"Right," Pete said.

"So that makes me *extra-special*!" She twirled, her backpack swinging wide, her shoulder-length blond hair fanning out behind.

Jane's fingers involuntarily tightened on her camera.

"You're extra-special every day, sweetheart."

Now Jane's chest tightened, as if her heart had swelled just a bit. A man who loved his daughter couldn't be all bad. Could he?

Rachel laughed and turned to Jane again. "Miss Loring said it's good to practice for very special things. Can you come and help me practice with the flowers?"

It took Jane a moment to respond. "Uh…well, yes. We could do that."

"Today?"

"Well...today or tomorrow."

"Promise?"

"Yes, I promise."

"Good!" Rachel grinned at Jane again, then tugged on Pete's hand. "I got the invitations, Daddy."

"She sure did," said Jed, holding up a small yellow envelope. "In fact, I'm the first to receive one. Isn't that right, Rachel?"

"Yep. I gave one to Grandpa Jed first, Daddy. Is that okay?"

"Fine by me," Pete said.

Rachel dug into her backpack. "Here's one for you. And one for Tina. And one for Jane." She handed them each an envelope. "And now I have to give one to Paz."

"She might be busy getting supper ready," Pete told her.

"But she told me she wants her invitation *right away*."

"Did she?"

As he looked down at his daughter, Pete's half smile softened his features. His dark eyelashes highlighted his hazel eyes. Jane's fingers tightened on the camera again. It took a conscious effort to relax her grip.

"C'mon, Rachel," Jed said. "Let's go see Paz."

"I'll go with you." Tina stepped from behind the registration desk. "Robbie ran right into the kitchen to talk to Abuela when he and Rachel came home."

Before Jane could blink, she found herself alone in the lobby with Pete, who stood watching his daughter skip down the hallway. In profile, his eyelashes looked long and thick, his lips firm, his jaw solid and beginning to darken with stubble.

She wondered what she would have done if he had taken her up on the suggestion to climb into the bubble bath.

But of course, she would have gone for the best angle—while hoping her shaking hands wouldn't destroy the results.

At photo shoots, she sometimes saw people—female and male—wearing nothing but scraps of clothing. She was used to that. She saw what the camera showed her, filtered through the lens. Yet simply the thought of seeing Pete Brannigan undressed seemed to be a whole other story.

Maybe it was that sexy shadow on his jaw…or the light brown hair that turned golden in sunlight… Or maybe it was his broad shoulders and muscular chest…his sculpted arms and flat abs… Whatever it was, the man had what it took to grace the cover of any magazine.

He turned his head and caught her looking at him.

Normally, that wouldn't have bothered her, but after their close encounter and his attempt to rattle her in the suite, she felt the need to say something. "It's only an occupational hazard."

"Staring at me?"

"In your dreams, cowboy. No, not you. Not even men specifically. Faces. Male or female. Cats, dogs, you name it."

"Even horses."

She nodded. "Even horses. Like Daffodil. And I wasn't staring at you. I was observing."

"There's a difference?"

"Yes." She reached for her camera, then realized she still held the envelope his daughter had given her. She raised it to his eye level. "Rachel's a little young to be handing out wedding invitations, isn't she? And if it's for Tina's wedding, I thought the bride had that covered."

He laughed, more at the mention of his daughter, she was sure, than in amusement over her comment, yet the sudden lightness in his expression sent a rush of pleasure through her.

"Not a wedding," he said. "It's for her kindergarten graduation."

"Oh." Silly, but the thought of being invited made her feel "extra-special." She smiled.

To her surprise, he frowned. "It's not till after the wedding, and you and Andi will be gone. Don't worry about making excuses to Rachel. I'll explain to her why you can't come."

"Maybe I'd rather make my *own* 'excuses.'" There she went, allowing him to push her buttons again. Attending a kindergarten graduation would be the last thing she'd ever find on her agenda, but she couldn't let Pete believe he could make her decisions for her. "I've been good about speaking up for myself ever since I was a kid."

"Yeah, I'd noticed."

"You're not going to let the past go, are you?"

"Past, present. Doesn't seem to matter when it is—you like to argue."

"And you don't?"

"Nope. I just like to keep the conversation going till I get the last word."

She laughed. "Rachel seems to take after you."

"Not enough." Suddenly, he was frowning again.

"She does bear a striking resemblance to your wife."

"Ex-wife." He clamped his teeth together so hard, a muscle in his jaw throbbed.

"Ex-wife."

"And let's just leave her out of this, all right?"

Now she was the one to frown. "Is that what you say when Rachel asks about her?"

"What I tell my daughter is none—" His jaws clamped shut again.

None of your business.

"Let's just stick to business," he added, "like my ex-wife does."

His flat statement only confirmed her thought about what he had wanted to say. And he was right. His conversations with his daughter were not her concern. Neither was his obviously rocky relationship with his ex-wife.

"And," he said, "I'd just as soon you not throw out any empty promises to Rachel, either."

"Empty promises?"

"About helping her with the flowers."

"That wasn't an empty promise."

"No? You didn't sound interested, but you plan to follow through? Because you can't just say something like that to a kid Rachel's age and not expect her to take it to heart."

He turned to go down the hallway. She stared after him in surprise.

No wonder the poor man had problems in his relationships.

PETE STOOD BY the corral watching Rachel run across the yard to the house. He knew his housekeeper would come to the porch to acknowledge his daughter's arrival home, as she always did.

Inside the corral, Cole and another of the ranch hands were finishing up a riding lesson with a couple of guests from the hotel.

Near the barn, the stable hand, Eddie, stood grooming Bingo. They kept the Shetland for the smallest kids, including Jed's great-grandson, Robbie.

Rachel gave him a quick wave and went inside the house with Sharon.

He thought of Jane's question about what he told his

daughter, then winced as he recalled his response. It sure wouldn't win him any prizes for politeness.

Maybe he ought to thank her for the question, since his reply would put some distance between them again. Distance he definitely needed, especially after her half-hearted agreement to help Rachel "practice with the flowers." Her protest to him that she was not making an empty promise had sounded just as weak.

The hotel guests also waved to him on their way to the hotel. In return, he tipped his Stetson.

Cole had handed his reins to the other wrangler and walked up to join Pete. He nodded in the direction of the guests. "They've come a long way this week. And they're talking about another visit to the ranch soon."

"Jed will be happy to hear it."

"I see Rachel got home okay."

"Yeah. Robbie, too," he added, knowing Cole would ask about his and Tina's son. He smiled. "Rachel's all excited about her graduation."

"So I've been hearing. Sounds like it's going to be a big production."

"Not nearly as big a deal as the wedding."

"The ladies *are* going to town with it, aren't they?" Cole shook his head. "But that's what it's about, I guess. Lucky for us, we just have to get dressed and show up."

"Sounds like the voice of experience," Pete said with a laugh.

"That would be you, not me."

"Yeah." Not such a great experience, as it turned out.

He led the way to the barn.

Not long after he'd hired Sharon, his divorce had come through. Marina hadn't requested regular visitation with the kids. She hadn't even wanted custody, claiming it would be better for him to have full charge, since she never knew when her schedule would take her out of the country.

Her rise to fame had been the kind of overnight success story heard about only in the news. Well, now she was someone making that news, the latest glamour girl whose face and figure showed up on cover after magazine cover. And he couldn't fault her for being happy about having the life she'd always wanted.

Too bad she hadn't bothered telling him she'd wanted that life before they'd married and started raising a couple of kids. Not that he ever had or ever would regret having Rachel and Eric.

He loved his kids. And though his marriage had fallen apart, he sure as hell planned to hold his little family together.

Inside the barn, Cole said, "I've got the order we picked up waiting in your office, all but a couple of items on back order."

"Some of it needs to go out to the supply cabins." They went down the list together, discussing what should stay in the barn and what they should transfer. "Let's load this up now, and you can take it out first thing in the morning."

Cole nodded. "Think you'll be around, or are you going to be busy over at the hotel again? I've been hearing about that, too."

"From who?" he demanded.

"Jed mentioned it. And he and Jane were talking about it over breakfast. With the renovations partially done, she said she intended to get some of her pictures taken."

"Tina's still hoping to have everything finished up by late fall?"

"Yeah. If she can push the contractors to move any

faster. But that seems about as likely as pulling out the back teeth of a bull with lockjaw."

"I wouldn't want her job dealing with them. You and the boys give me enough grief."

"Ha. And what about Jane?"

"She'll be done with her pictures soon, and I'll be back here, where I belong." End of story. He lifted a supply carton from the floor.

"I'll bring the truck around to the back," Cole volunteered.

"Sounds good," he agreed, happy to change the subject.

He didn't want to talk about Jane. Despite all the strikes against her, he'd thought of her much too often. Worse, he was having a heck of a time getting images of her out of his head.

Maybe he'd just stayed away from women too long.

Since the divorce, he hadn't dated or even brought anyone new around his kids. In fact, he'd pretty much kept himself to himself. He had no plans to jump into another relationship. But, for his kids' sake, he couldn't rule out the idea of marrying again someday. He just needed to find the right woman to make his family complete.

No way was a smart-mouthed city slicker like Jane Garland the right woman to be a mom to his kids.

And no way was she the woman for him…no matter how much he wanted her.

Chapter Four

June might be a great month for a wedding—if you liked weddings—but as he'd futilely reminded Jed, it was also a busy one on the ranch. Too busy to spend an afternoon or even a few hours playing assistant to a perfectionist photographer. Yet he'd returned for another day of taking Jane's directions, and this time, he'd looked forward to that more than he should.

She hadn't stood still all morning. He wondered if she was as rattled as he was over that moment on the back porch.

For the third time in ten minutes, he rearranged a table and chairs in the Hitching Post's dining room.

"That's good," she said. "A few more shots ought to do it."

"For this room?"

"For the day. Tina and Grandpa should be back from the airport soon."

He nodded. Early that morning, Jed had told him they would be picking up his middle granddaughter and her kids.

Jane started in on the routine that had become familiar to him by now, standing at one side of the room, then slowly covering the area, clicking the camera as she went along.

The sound of her heels on the hardwood floor brought his attention to her leather ankle boots. Black leather, of course. From there, his gaze naturally went to shapely calves and then slim thighs. A long-tailed button-down shirt hid the rest of her curves. Unfortunately, that didn't do a thing to rein in his imagination.

He wanted to move closer, to undo that shirt one button at a time. At the very least, he wanted to get her talking again. He took a couple of steps forward just as she backed up, walking directly into him. Instantly, he realized how far his imagination had taken him and how quickly his body had followed. He hoped she hadn't been able to notice.

When she turned to face him, he racked his brain for something halfway intelligent to say. "We'd better hurry this up."

"Hurry?"

"Yeah. With Jed and your cousins coming back, anyone could interrupt us at any time." The thought of having anything *to* interrupt got him hot all over. *Dang.* He had to forget this crazy desire for her. Or do something to satisfy it.

She stepped away. "Just a few more shots."

He laughed. "I've heard that one before." He settled into a chair at a table for two near the wall. Maybe the space would help him cool down a bit. "Must cost you a fortune in film."

She shook her head. "This camera's digital. That means it goes straight from the camera to the computer."

"Didn't know you could do that," he said.

She must not have picked up on his teasing. Eyebrows shooting up in surprise, she glanced at him. "Come on. You've got a camera phone, haven't you?"

"Yeah." He shrugged. "I've never used it to take a picture, and I don't mind saying—"

"—I'm danged proud of it," she finished. "I could just hear that coming. But don't tell me you don't use a computer."

He couldn't honestly say that but wanted to agree, just to see her reaction.

"You would have to," she went on. "You must deal with budgets and payroll and other reports for the ranch."

"Tina generally takes care of all those."

She took the chair opposite his. Her camera sounded hollow as she set it on the tabletop. "You're telling me your fingers never touch a keyboard?" she asked. "Not even for email?"

"From time to time," he admitted. "Not more than I can help it." He ran his fingertips along the surface of the table. "Feel this." He took her hand and laid it flat on the table, his fingers covering hers. She looked quickly at him, but didn't pull away.

"This was once a tree," he said, "something alive and breathing. Something natural, not like the plastic and metal in that camera of yours." She freed her hand and reached for the hunk of metal again, as if the small lump of man-made material were formed of solid gold. As if she couldn't function without it. He shrugged. "I prefer wood and wool to computers or video games. Or any kind of electronics."

"Oh. Well…why stop there? Why not give up electricity altogether? You could have Rachel do her homework by candlelight." She laughed. Her eyes sparkled. "How do you feel about indoor plumbing, by the way? There's plenty of wide-open space out here to set up a few outhouses."

"Very funny." He didn't care that she definitely hadn't

caught on to his teasing about the camera. But her tone hit too close to home and his father's frequent remarks.

"It was meant to be." She shook her head. "Even you can't be as out of touch with the modern world as all that."

Way too close to home. "'Out of touch.' Now, where have I heard that before?"

"I don't know. Where?"

"From my dad. It's one of his favorite expressions when he's talking to me. And when he really wants to make an impression, he reminds me I could have had a better career." He shook his head. "He doesn't get that I'll never want a job other than being a rancher."

"Ah… I'm beginning to see where all this is coming from."

"All this what?"

"This resistance. This rebellion. This 'I'm not doing it and you can't make me' defense." She laughed. "Yet you call *me* stubborn?"

"I'm not defensive. And as I already told you, ma'am, I'm not shy." He ran his fingertips down a strand of her shiny black hair. "I'm just a good ol' cowboy, a rancher at home on the range. Anyhow, what's wrong with good, old-fashioned cowboy values?"

"Maybe some of them are outdated, just as your father said."

"I'd rather talk about your dad. And you."

She shrugged. "Why not? I've got nothing to hide."

His heart tripped a beat at the image *that* statement brought to mind. Nobody in his right mind would walk away from an offer like this one. Maybe that was why he planned to take her up on it. To prove he *wasn't* crazy and to show he was in control of his emotions—even if he couldn't swear to either of those at the moment.

"I already know where you get your streak of perfectionism. How'd you get to be so independent—growing up with a dad in the service?"

"Not just in. He's a five-star general."

"I'll bet that gave you some perks."

"Maybe. But there are drawbacks to being a military brat, too."

"Such as?"

"If any kid didn't show up for class, the entire Army base heard about it."

"Bet that would go over well. Your dad was strict with you?"

"Oh, yeah. He wouldn't let me date until I was seventeen."

"Sounds lenient to me. I'm thinking Rachel should wait till she's twenty-five."

She laughed.

The sound drew him to her. He leaned across the table, until only a few inches separated them. "So, tell me about this first date."

"What do you want to know?"

At the sound of running footsteps approaching the dining room, they both sat back. He had no time to answer her question. Probably the best thing for them both, considering the direction his thoughts were headed.

He turned his attention to the doorway. He'd wager the footsteps meant the school bus had arrived, bringing Rachel home from her kindergarten class and Robbie from his preschool. Seconds later, he won the bet when both kids ran into the room.

"Hi, Daddy!" Rachel called. "Hi, Jane! Can you take my picture? Like this?" She slung her backpack over one shoulder and put her free hand on her hip.

He frowned. More than a few times over the past couple of days, she had talked about Jane and her camera.

He didn't want to see that trend continue. Didn't like the idea of his daughter growing too attached. Soon, Jane would leave again to go off on her travels, and Rachel would feel abandoned.

Before she could respond, he said, "Not now, Rachel."

"I don't mind," Jane said.

"See, Daddy?"

"And," he went on steadily, "I think you and I had better head for our house. Jane and Robbie are going to have company."

"I know. Andi's coming today. And Trey and Missy."

"We need to let Sharon know you're home."

"Huh-uh, we don't!" Her giggle sounded triumphant. "Sharon's in the kitchen with Paz. When everybody gets here, we're having a tea party. Paz made sopaipillas and cookies."

"Chocolate cookies," Robbie said. He had a real fondness for chocolate—and a real tough time getting a word in edgewise whenever Rachel was around.

Another thing he'd need to talk to her about.

"I hear Grandpa!" Robbie announced. He ran from the room.

"C'mon, Jane." Rachel took her hand. "We have to go say hi. You, too, Daddy." She led Jane toward the doorway, leaving him in their dust.

DURING THE "PARTY" to welcome Andi and her kids back to the ranch, Pete continued to fight his uneasiness. Rachel's sudden attachment to Jane almost rivaled his fascination with the woman.

For both reasons, he hadn't planned to stick around, but Jed insisted. The boss urged him to have a cup of coffee, then included him in the conversation about the changes happening to the hotel. Worse, Jed had made suggestions that only increased Jane's need for help with her photos.

Somehow, in everyone's eyes but his own, he'd gone from lowly photographer's assistant to a necessary member of the hotel revitalization team.

When Jed had come up with his plans for the renovation, Tina accepted responsibility for hiring the contractors. Andi agreed to hire the folks who would take care of the food, flowers and whatever else the hotel needed for wedding receptions and other events. Jane…well, he knew what Jane was handling, along with her primary job of driving him crazy with wanting her.

She sat a few seats away from him at the center table in the dining room. The wrought-iron fixture above the table gave her already shiny hair an almost metallic glow. High-tech hairstyle to match her high-tech toys.

"Pete?"

He started. The raised voice and the stares from a couple of the others at the table made it apparent Jed had spoken to him more than once. "Sorry, boss. Just making a mental note to check on Starlight when I leave here." It was the best he could come up with.

Andi sat in the chair beside his. She smiled at him. "I'll have to take a walk out to the stables to say hello."

On her visits to Garland Ranch, she spent a lot of time around the barn and the corral—certainly more than Jane ever had. While he couldn't call Andi a friend, at least they had a cordial relationship. And now, unfortunately, they had more in common than an interest in horses. Recently widowed, she was a single parent, too, with a son a couple of years younger than Rachel and a newborn daughter.

When the conversation shifted, she turned to him and said quietly, "Eric's getting big. It's been such a short time since our last visit, but I already see so many differences in him."

"They sure grow fast, don't they?"

"They sure do. And Rachel," she murmured, "is getting prettier by the minute."

"Don't let her hear you say that. I've already got a diva on my hands." It took all his effort to force a grin.

His daughter had taken the chair on one side of Jane. On Jane's other side, Sharon sat holding his son. Eric wrapped his chubby hand around Jane's long silver chains and gave them a tug, the way he reined in his toy pony-on-wheels. The way Pete himself had touched that chain just the day before, though with more restraint.

"Stop, Eric," Rachel demanded. "You'll break Jane's necklace."

Instead, his son reached out with his free hand, as if wanting Jane to take him into her arms.

"I said stop, Eric."

Pete looked at his daughter.

"He's not—" Jane began.

"Rachel," he said quietly.

After a quick glance at him, she mumbled "Okay, Daddy" and slumped back in her seat. The set of her mouth told him she was gearing up for a pout.

Evidently, Sharon noticed the warning sign, too. "Much as I hate to break up the party, some of us need to leave." Gently, she uncurled his son's fingers from the necklace. "Eric hasn't had his nap, have you, sweetie? And, Rachel, come along. You've got to help me get some vegetables ready, or your daddy won't have any supper."

"I'm good with vegetables." All smiles now, Rachel looked at Jane. "You can come, too. I'll let you snap the beans. That's the most fun part."

Jane smiled. "I—"

"You run along," he told Rachel. "Go with Sharon, the way she asked you to."

"Maybe another time, Rachel," Jane said. "I need to visit with Andi."

As Sharon left the room with the kids, he swallowed a relieved sigh, happy to have her create some space between his family and Jane. He turned to Jed. "I plan to be up in the northeast pastures with the boys most of tomorrow."

"Fine," his boss said.

"Fine with me, too," his other boss said. Jane's mouth curved into a half smile as if she somehow knew the effort it took to keep his expression blank. "I'll be in Santa Fe anyway."

"For our final fittings," Tina reminded him.

"Right." His daughter needed to go along. "I'll make sure Sharon has Rachel over here on time tomorrow morning."

Not quite as happy now, he left the dining room.

He and the bride-to-be had agreed it was a good thing Andi's later arrival meant postponing the trip to Santa Fe until the weekend. This eliminated the need to excuse their kids from school. With Rachel's graduation so close, he and Tina both knew how she would react to the idea of missing out on anything.

The trouble now was, he didn't like his daughter spending the day with Jane or the way even Eric seemed to have taken such a shine to her.

Maybe they'd somehow picked up on his feelings about the woman. Almost against his better judgment, he found himself drawn to her. And with every minute they spent together, his willpower took more of a beating.

THE NEXT AFTERNOON, Jane eyed herself critically in the triple mirror at the bridal shop in Santa Fe.

"You look great," Tina told her.

Tina and Rachel had already completed their fittings, and now the three bridesmaids would be taking their turn. Bright colors weren't her thing, but even she had to admit the royal blue halter-top gown didn't look bad with her dark hair.

She laughed. "I guess I'd never have stood a chance of getting you to agree to a black-and-white wedding."

"Not with Ally around," Tina assured her.

"You've got that right, *chica*." The maid of honor looked stunning in a hot-pink, off-the-shoulder gown, but she tossed her long black curls and gave a theatrical moan. "*I* wanted to wear purple and orange."

"And I put my foot down about that."

"*Stomped* it down, you mean," Ally grumbled.

They all laughed. As they waited for the seamstress to return to the fitting room, they continued talking about the upcoming wedding.

Jane's attention drifted to one corner of the room, where Rachel and Robbie were sitting far enough away to prevent their overhearing the conversation. A game board lay open on the floor between them, and Rachel seemed to be explaining the rules to Robbie.

She smiled. Sharon had brought Rachel to the Hitching Post early this morning, and the little girl had sat beside her at breakfast. In the ranch's big SUV, Rachel had worked her way to a seat next to Jane, too.

Watching Rachel made her think of Rachel's daddy and the way he acted every time she was around the child. What could he possibly have against her talking to his daughter? He seemed as strict with the girl as her own father had been with her. Maybe for that reason alone, her sympathy went to Rachel.

Still, she couldn't deny she had other feelings for Pete. The memory of his touching her hand and her hair sent a pleasurable tremor down her spine. To her dismay, when she caught sight of her reflection in the mirror, her cheeks had turned pink.

Beside her, Ally leaned closer to the mirror and adjusted the bodice of her gown. "I think I'm going to give up eating this week."

"Then you'd have to come back for another fitting," Tina reminded her.

"Oh…that's true. Maybe I'll just skip desserts." Ally glanced at Jane.

Glad for the chance to redirect her thoughts, Jane laughed.

They had planned to have dinner here in Santa Fe. Before the ride, they had all met for a quick lunch in town. At SugarPie's, Cowboy Creek's bakery and sandwich shop, the two of them had learned they shared a love of sweets.

"You're on your own with that idea," Jane said. "The other day, I thought about sacrificing dessert and realized I'd rather give up my main course—although I'm not sure about that now, either. Paz's cooking is too delicious. And I can't wait to get to SugarPie's again. Sugar's corned beef sandwich is as good as any New York deli's."

"Is it enough to make you stay in Cowboy Creek?" Tina asked.

Jane laughed. "Sorry, nothing's *that* good."

"Speaking of giving up," Andi said, "have you fired your assistant yet?"

She froze for a moment, then pretended to be inspecting her dress more closely in the mirror. "No, I haven't. Why?"

"I'm not so sure Pete likes taking orders from you."

"First of all, Andi, I don't give orders. And he's fine about doing things for me."

"Maybe he'd like to do even more for you," Ally murmured.

"Watch it, girl, or I'll steal your dessert tonight." Jane looked at all three women and settled her gaze on her cousin Tina. Unlike Andi with her teasing and Ally with her over-the-top ideas, quiet, reserved Tina could always be counted on to tell the truth without embellishment. "What's going on?"

Tina smiled. "I think Andi means Pete's distraction when Jed was talking to him in the dining room yesterday. Ally was probably taking a wild guess about what Pete wants."

The maid of honor rolled her eyes.

"Why should his distraction have something to do with me?" Jane said. And why did even the thought of it make goose bumps race down her bare arms? "He's probably got a lot on his mind. He's told me—more than once—how busy it is on the ranch around this time."

She had mentioned that to her grandfather and suggested he have one of his other cowhands help her, but Jed didn't seem at all concerned about her tying up his manager's time. Instantly, she had made up her mind to ditch her guilt over taking Pete away from his job. If only she could just as easily ignore that she enjoyed spending that time with him.

Tina nodded. "That's true—the ranch is busy. But I wouldn't lose any sleep over it. We have plenty of staff."

"And now there won't be any guests at the hotel for a while," Andi said.

Despite Tina's protests, Jed had insisted on blocking out the coming two weeks on the hotel calendar. He'd said that, other than dealing with the contractors, he wanted the bride-to-be free to focus on the wedding and her visit with Jane and Andi and their parents.

Jane smiled. "I'll remember that in case Pete says something about his workload. And I already told him if he didn't want to help, he could send a replacement." Which had led to their conversation about a bubble bath and his eventual declaration, *Honey, I'm not shy about anything.*

Even thinking about that made her breath catch. Just how could he prove that claim? And, given the chance, would he?

"That's my point," Ally said with a grin. "Maybe he *does* want to help."

"Ally," Tina said warningly.

"What? Come on, *chica*. Marina's been out of the man's life for a couple of years now. And you might not drop in at Cowboy Creek's hottest—and only—nightspot, but I do, and I can tell you there's never a sign of Pete at the Cantina."

"Sounds like a man ready for some female companionship."

Andi was only taking a turn at teasing, Jane knew. But she couldn't tease her cousin back or even get upset. Not when she looked at the dark circles beneath Andi's eyes. Not when she thought of all her cousin had lost. Andi, younger by just a few months, had been widowed less than a year ago, soon after she and her husband learned she was pregnant with their second child.

"Seriously," Andi asked Tina, "what happened with Pete and Marina?"

Jane looked in the mirror and adjusted the hem of her gown. The last thing she wanted was to give any of them the idea she cared about Pete. Being around the man only added some fun and a few fantasy-provoking moments to her life. That would soon end when she left the ranch. Still, that didn't stop her from remaining tuned in to the conversation.

"Nobody knows exactly what made them break up," Tina admitted. "Pete doesn't say much about it."

"We know one of the reasons things didn't work out with them, though. *Marina*," Ally emphasized, flipping the ends of her hair, "is more of a drama queen than I am."

The other two women laughed. Even Jane couldn't keep from smiling.

"And you know Pete," Ally went on. "He's such a straight-up, private kind of guy. Maybe he could handle Marina's drama when they were alone, but he sure hated it when she started playing out her scenes in public."

That sounded like more than just a private person's need for a quiet life. It seemed to be the reaction of a man who didn't want to deal with a flamboyant wife and who resented that wife's successful career.

"And that's it?" Andi asked Tina.

"Just about. Since their divorce, Marina hasn't come back to town."

"Not even to see her kids?" Andi's voice broke.

Jane frowned. Andi was still grieving over the loss of her husband. She certainly didn't need to be upset by thoughts of Pete's virtually motherless children.

She recalled what he had said about his ex-wife. Considering his attitude, she could see why the woman might not want to be around him.

Between his interruptions when she talked to his kids and his teasing over her perfectionism—a trait she preferred to call "attention to detail"—she should have found him irritating.

Instead, the challenge of their verbal sparring was rapidly turning into something more. There was just something about him, about his love for his kids, about his soft laugh and his rough yet gentle hands, that made her want to be near him.

For her own peace of mind, she *ought* to fire the man. Instead, she thought again of the way he'd pressed her hand and stroked her hair.

How could she tell him she didn't need his assistance? She could barely wait to see what he would do next.

Chapter Five

"As far as I can see, Jane and Pete are a mite slow at heating things up," Jed complained to Paz. He stood leaning against the kitchen counter near where she was working.

First Jane's arrival and then picking up Andi and her kids at the airport yesterday had kept him from having much opportunity for a quiet chat with Paz. With all the girls in Santa Fe that afternoon, the two of them were taking advantage of the chance to catch up.

"You expected to have a challenge, yes?" she asked.

"Yes. But I didn't know I'd have to work so hard at it."

He watched her shred another peeled potato. The potatoes would go into one of her specialties, a casserole that was always a hit at the Hitching Post's Sunday brunches.

She paused to look at him. "You knew Pete and Jane would need encouragement to spend time together."

"*Encouragement*'s not the word. A lasso and some baling wire might be in order here." He shook his head. "Pete keeps trying to get out of helping Jane, and even Jane suggested I might want to replace him. And yet, I believe I'm seeing some progress."

"Of course that's progress. If they push to get away from each other, that means they have a strong reaction. Right now, they think they don't like what they're feeling."

"Huh. And just what makes you so sure of this?"

"It happens all the time on my programs."

He laughed. "Yeah, I'll bet it does." Paz wasn't one to watch much television, but every weekday afternoon, she glued herself to the couch in her sitting room for the length of a couple of soap operas. He could understand that. The snippets he'd seen usually included as much action and excitement as any of the shoot-'em-up Westerns he preferred.

"Pete and Jane will be together Friday night at the rehearsal and Saturday at the wedding," she reminded him.

"Yeah, I know. But meanwhile we've got this week to get through."

"Your idea to have him help her with her pictures is a good one."

He nodded. "It is, isn't it? I'll just need to come up with ways to keep that going."

"If that doesn't work, tell Pete he should help out of respect for you. Later, he'll be glad you brought him together with Jane."

"That's true," he agreed, brightening. After all, those two were meant to be a matched set.

They just didn't know it yet.

IN A LULL after the Hitching Post's busy Sunday brunch, Jane followed Tina to the kitchen to see what help they could offer Paz. Maria, this morning's waitress, had already left for the day.

Andi, in riding gear, sat at the kitchen table cradling her daughter.

Tina was given the chore of loading the industrial-sized dishwasher, while Jane had the exciting job of folding the colorful napkins that were used in the dining room.

"This is probably the only thing I *can* help with besides boiling water." She loved her New York co-op and its bright and cheery kitchen, but she didn't spend much time there.

"You have to start somewhere," Tina said as she went to the sink.

"I suppose so."

"If Rachel can snap beans," Andi said, "you might be able to handle it."

"*Might?* Thanks for the vote of confidence, coz."

Andi laughed.

By the refrigerator, Paz turned to look their way. "You could stay here, Jane, and I would teach you to cook."

"Just like she's teaching me," Tina said.

Paz waved her hand. "You know more than you think."

"That's probably true, Abuela, but I've told you this before—you won't leave your kitchen long enough for me to find out."

They all laughed.

"Here's another vote of confidence," Andi said. "If you want to work on your domestic skills, try holding Missy for a while."

Before Jane could protest, Andi placed the infant into her arms. "You're taking a chance," she said. The mothering gene had skipped right over her and landed hard on her younger cousins. She loved their kids, but having a family wasn't on her agenda at the moment. "I know less about babies than I do about cooking."

Andi smiled. "You could learn that, too."

Jane looked down at the tiny warm bundle in her arms. She kissed Missy's soft cheek and inhaled the scent of fresh-washed baby blanket and powder. "She's precious."

"And you could have a baby of your own," Paz said.

Jane laughed. "Can't you just see that?"

"Yes, I can," Paz said seriously.

Finished drying her hands, Tina crossed the room. "Right now, *I* can have *this* baby. Andi promised I could watch Missy while she went for a ride."

With mixed reluctance and relief, Jane handed the child to her.

"Well, then." Andi stood. "Jane's now free to walk with me out to the corral."

Jane's breath caught. Luckily, Paz and Tina, both cooing over the baby, hadn't noticed. "What's the matter, coz? Have you forgotten the way?"

"Not at all." Andi's small smile said she had noticed Jane's reaction. "I just have a sudden craving for your company."

Jane faked a sigh. "Well, I guess if you can't do without me, I'll have to take that walk to the corral with you."

With any luck, she would get a glimpse of the rancher in charge.

They left through the door to the back porch and went down the stairs.

"Here we are," Andi said, her voice as bright as the sun overhead. "Just like old times, walking to the barn together."

Jane raised her eyebrows and looked at her.

Tina was the youngest of the three cousins. Jane was the oldest. With just a few months' difference between herself and Andi, they had been close growing up, though they saw each other only when their parents' vacations coincided.

"Yes," Jane said. "Here we are. And what exactly are you leading up to with that cat-and-canary grin?"

"Nothing but giving you the opportunity to talk. You look like you need it. And now's our chance. So tell me, what's happening between you and Pete?"

"Why should there be anything going on?"

"Oh, Jane. That's as bad as the line you used yesterday. 'Why should his distraction have something to do with me?'" Andi mimicked. "Come on—admit it. You've had a thing for him for years."

She looked ahead of them up the path. Eddie, the stable hand, led a fully saddled horse from the barn. As Jed had cleared the hotel for the week except for family and wedding guests, more than likely the horse was for Andi to ride.

"Yeah," Jane said finally. "I've got a need to aggravate Pete."

"And I'm sure you've done a great job of it. But don't tell me there's not something else beyond that."

"So, a long time ago, we each had a schoolgirl crush on one of Grandpa's ranch hands. Neither of those crushes lasted."

"No, they didn't." Andi's suddenly emotionless tone told Jane she was thinking of the man she had gone on to marry.

She, on the other hand, had just gone on with life.

She looked across the yard to the barn again.

When she saw Pete standing in the doorway, her pulse quickened. He watched their approach, removing his Stetson to run his hand through his hair. The light brown strands picked up golden highlights from the sun.

Jane's breath caught.

She hadn't realized she'd inhaled so sharply with pleasure until she heard her cousin laugh.

"I was only half-right yesterday," Andi said. "Maybe you and Pete are *both* ready for some companionship." She looked over at her. "You said yourself you gave him the option to send someone else to help. He didn't take you up on it, did he?"

"No." A tiny shot of satisfaction made her fight to hide

a smile. "But that doesn't mean anything. He's probably just glad to get a break from his ranching duties."

"Uh-huh. And *you'd* probably be glad to get your hands on your hot rancher, just the way Tina has."

"He's not mine."

"Maybe he could be."

At the thought, her pulse picked up again, but she shook her head. "We don't have a lot in common, Andi. Besides, he's got a family keeping him here, and I need to stay on the move."

"You could stop moving. Take those cooking lessons from Paz," Andi teased.

"As if."

As ridiculous as the idea was, she couldn't help but thank Andi for trying. Just as she couldn't help the way her heart began to thump when Pete waved his hat in greeting. Then he turned and entered the barn.

She wasn't about to chase him, not after Andi's teasing and especially not with Eddie standing in the doorway watching Andi get into the saddle.

Instead, she rested her arms on the corral fence until Andi trotted her horse away from the barn. She watched until both horse and rider made one speck in the distance.

After another few moments, she shot a glance toward the barn, then finally walked back to the Hitching Post alone.

EVEN RANCH MANAGERS had to have a day off, Jane admitted when the rest of Sunday passed without a sign of Pete. She hadn't talked to him since Friday, hadn't seen him since that morning. Both meetings seemed a very long time ago. She felt worse when she recalled how he had turned away when she and Andi approached.

This afternoon, though she might temporarily have lost an assistant, she seemed to have gained a shadow.

Rachel, Robbie and Andi's son, Trey, had settled down on the sitting room floor to play under the watchful eye of their doting great-grandfather and, often, Andi or Tina.

Every time Jane entered the room, Rachel found a reason to come sit beside her, as she had done on their trip to Santa Fe the day before. Sometimes, she would bring an update on a board game. Other times, she would show off one of the horses the kids were playing with in a cardboard corral.

"Looks like you've made a conquest of that one," Jed said on her next visit to the room. He sat cradling Andi's sleeping infant to his chest.

Jane sank onto the couch opposite him. Considering the way Pete reacted every time she spoke to his daughter, she couldn't imagine him calmly taking the news of Rachel's attentions.

"You look good with a little one by your side," Jed added.

She shook her head. "Don't start, Grandpa. Tina and Andi have already given you a few great-grands to keep you occupied."

"Always room in my arms for another one."

"Always room in your heart, too, I know." She smiled. "But no room in my life yet." And maybe there never would be.

"Haven't seen Pete around here today."

She stiffened. "No."

"The boys are still working the northeast pastures. Gotta get them done before they can move on."

"So that's—" She stopped, mentally kicking herself for the slip Jed was too smart not to notice.

He nodded. "That's why he's not around."

From across the room, Rachel spotted her, waved and began to get to her feet.

"Sounds like you two are making some good progress," he added. When she stared at him, he continued quickly, "With the pictures, I mean. Now, don't forget what I said the other day about readying up one of those cabins."

"I won't." Truthfully, until he had mentioned them, she had forgotten all about the small cabins on the far side of the hotel. They were being refurbished as part of the Hitching Post's rejuvenation, and the contractors had finished their work in one of them.

"The suites upstairs are nice," he continued, "and they'll do fine, too, but we can't have a website without showing off those honeymoon hideaways, now, can we."

"Jane's going to take pictures in the cabins, Grandpa Jed?" Rachel hopped up on the couch beside Jane. "Can I go with you, Jane? I never get to go in the cabins. You can take some pictures of *me*, too. And I can *help* you."

Jane smiled. A shadow and a new assistant, all in one. If only she could hold that much interest for Rachel's daddy.

Not likely. Just because she was fascinated by the man, she couldn't fool herself into thinking he was genuinely wrapped up in her.

As she settled back against the couch, Rachel held up a toy horse. "I like this one best, because it's a Shetland, like Bingo. I learned to ride on Bingo." She leaned forward to whisper, "Sometimes I let Robbie have this one. Because Miss Loring says we have to share."

"Miss Loring gives you lots of good advice, doesn't she?"

Rachel nodded. "My daddy and Sharon and Grandpa

Jed do, too. But *they* don't give me a time-out if I don't remember."

Jane looked toward Jed, whose huge grin made her struggle doubly hard to hold back her laugh. "What do they do?"

"Well, Sharon tells me I need to stop and think two times about how I would feel if somebody didn't share with me."

"That's good advice, too."

"Yeah. And Grandpa Jed says—" Rachel took a deep breath and attempted to mimic Jed's deep voice "'—I'll tell you flat-out straight, little girl, sometimes you have to con-…con-…'"

"Concede," Jed supplied.

"'—concede.' That means give up, right?"

"It can," he agreed. "But it can also mean to let go for just a while."

Exactly what she should do with her fantasies of Pete.

When Missy squirmed in Jed's arms and he turned his attention to the baby, she focused on Rachel. "And…your father?" she asked quietly under Missy's cries. "What does he say when you don't remember to share?"

Rachel laughed. "He says I'm an apple falling out of a tree. Or something like that." She looked down to stroke her pony's mane. When she looked up again at Jane, she was wide-eyed and unsmiling. "And then he just looks sad."

Chapter Six

Late Monday afternoon, Pete reined in near the quiet corral and dismounted to lead his horse across the yard. When he gave a loud whistle, Eddie came running to take the reins from him.

As boy and horse walked away, Pete turned to Jed, who stood in the barn doorway as if he'd been set there during spring planting and had been sending down roots ever since.

"Almost finished with the sweep of the southeast pastures?" the boss asked.

He nodded. Already, yesterday, they had moved on to the new area. From his viewpoint, Jed's decision to close the hotel to guests had worked in the ranch's favor this week, freeing up all of his men. "We'll be done with these pastures in the coming day or so. Then we'll move the herd and go on to the next."

"You'll have everything squared away by the end of the week, won't you?"

"Before that." He grinned. "The boys and I are taking Cole to town on Thursday to celebrate his last days as a free man. They've all already warned me they won't be in shape for any hard riding on Friday."

"Cole's friends, too?"

Cole's best man and another of the ushers were traveling in from Texas. "Yeah, he says they'll get in Thursday afternoon."

"And I expect them all to be sober for the rehearsal dinner on Friday."

"Can't speak for them, Jed, but you know I won't have trouble holding my head up." His nights out on the town had always been low-key and far between anyhow, but they'd virtually ended once Rachel had come along. He'd much preferred spending his free time with his baby girl.

"Good." Jed laughed. "If the best man runs into trouble, we might need you to step in."

"Let's hope it doesn't come to that." He shoved his work gloves into his back pockets. "I'd better go along and take a look at Starlight."

"And then mosey on over to the house, would you? Jane's upstairs in one of the suites."

"Sure."

Luckily, with the women gone to Santa Fe on Saturday and his long hours on the ranch yesterday, he'd had a break from running around after her. From the stress of denying his own instincts and maybe taking unfair advantage of hers.

After a nod to Jed, he returned to the barn just the way he had done yesterday when he'd seen Jane and Andi approach. From a distance, the two women didn't look related. Andi, with her long blond hair, had worn a white blouse and beige jeans with her brown riding boots. Jane made a stark contrast.

He seriously didn't like her addiction to black clothing, but he would have given anything to walk up to her and touch her dark hair again. He'd had to walk away, go back to the barn and to his job, or risk making a fool of himself in front of his stable hand and Andi.

He had hoped today's equally long day would have

given him another reprieve. There his luck had run out. So had his ability to resist her. His ride home had been filled with thoughts and images of her.

Spending another few photo sessions with her would be a small price to pay in return for everything Jed had given him. Yet he still didn't get why the boss had him helping her with jobs one of the ranch hands could easily tackle.

Unfortunately, that wasn't all he didn't understand.

What was more puzzling was he couldn't figure out why he was more interested in Jane than he'd ever been in any woman.

More often than not, she stayed behind her camera as if it were a protective shield, making him wonder why she needed the defense. At times, her comments seemed at odds with her wry smile; other times, her laugh left her mouth soft and her eyes gleaming. And then there were the clothes she wore, the leg-hugging pants paired with loose-fitting black shirts, as if she wanted to hide all those curves he still managed to see every time she shifted.

He shifted now at the sudden tightness below his belt—a reaction he'd gotten accustomed to since taking on the role of Jane's assistant. A purely healthy response to a completely unexpected sexual attraction. Forget denying and worrying. They ought to give in once and for all. Then they could get over the attraction.

"WHEN I GO get Paz's necklaces, will you take my picture, Jane?" Wearing a blouse she had borrowed from Jane, Rachel stood in front of the floor-length mirror in one of the honeymoon suites.

"Of course."

"Good."

This afternoon, as soon as the school bus driver dropped Rachel and Robbie in front of the hotel, Rachel had come in search of Jane. If her daddy was here, he would have promptly sent her home, Jane knew. But she hadn't seen him, Rachel had begged to stay, and a call to Sharon had resulted in the woman's wholehearted approval of the plan.

"And when you finish your work, can you play a game with me?"

Rachel's enthusiasm made her smile. "I think I can manage that."

"Good," the little girl repeated. She glanced at herself in the mirror. "My hair is just like Andi's."

"Yes, it is." Jane turned her attention back to the plate of strawberries she was arranging on the dresser.

Somehow, she had become Rachel's best buddy. For the rest of the afternoon yesterday, the little girl had played at the Hitching Post. Whenever Jane had gone back to the sitting room, Rachel had continued to hover close by.

Pete, on the other hand, hadn't come near her or the hotel. She hadn't seen him yet today, either. To her dismay, she felt another twinge of disappointment. She had no other verbal sparring partner here on the ranch, and though Pete might be a pain to work with, he kept her on her conversational toes. And, if she had to be honest, he had an effect on other parts of her body, too. Two small touches, yet the memories—combined with her fantasies—were more than enough to make her flush.

How could such an irritating man be so darned attractive?

From the corner of her eye, she watched his little girl turn and twist to check her reflection in the mirror, the way they had all done at the bridal shop on Saturday. "Look at my hair," Rachel said. "It's just like my mama's, too."

Which meant wavy, blond and beautiful, and nothing

like Jane's straight, shoulder-length black bob. She didn't need Rachel's input to know that.

Pete's ex-wife—just plain "Marina" to her fans in name but definitely not plain in appearance—had taken the modeling world by storm. Her face and figure had already appeared on some of the most coveted magazine covers and most widely viewed websites in that world. A friend of Jane's, on assignment in Paris, had seen Marina grace the runway at a prominent fashion show and had raved about how the camera loved her.

"Do you think my mama's gonna visit me soon?"

Jane froze. She wasn't equipped for this conversation. She wasn't the person Rachel should talk to. But here they were, with the question still unanswered. Carefully, she added two champagne glasses to her arrangement on the dresser and just as gently said, "I'm not sure when your mom will come to visit. Maybe you should ask your father."

"No. I ask him and ask him—"

And just how did Pete react to that?

"—but he never tells me. Sharon won't tell me, either."

"Well…maybe they don't know."

"Then they should find out." Rachel stared up at her and added solemnly, "Miss Loring says it's okay to ask questions. She says if we don't, we won't learn the answers."

She smiled. "Miss Loring is right again."

"But not now. I don't *have* any answers." Rachel sighed. "I think Mama forgot all about us." The tears in her eyes broke Jane's heart.

Obviously, the little girl was starved for her mother's attention.

If she, without a single nurturing instinct in her body, could understand that, why couldn't Pete?

PETE TRUDGED THROUGH the Hitching Post's lobby and up the wide staircase. He wished he had already paid his debt to Jed in full. He wished he had the strength to stay away from Jane. He'd tried yesterday by returning to the barn, but this was a new day and he couldn't fight the urge to be with her.

As Jed had said, she was in the bedroom of one of the honeymoon suites.

She wore the contemplative look he'd come to know and distrust, considering it usually resulted in him moving heavy furniture around or standing forever with a prop in his hands. He'd also come to appreciate that it gave them more time together.

She was staring at a couple of glasses and a plate of strawberries sitting on the dresser. The sight of her so near the king-size bed gave him ideas he didn't need to be having. When he strode into the room, he resolutely turned his back on the bed.

"Well, howdy, stranger," Jane drawled.

"Missed me, huh?"

For a moment, she looked disconcerted, as if he'd hit the mark and she didn't care for that. His certainty she had thought about him filled him with satisfaction.

She shrugged. "Let's say I felt your absence, the way you feel residual pain after a splinter's been removed from your finger."

He laughed. "In other words, my memory stays with you. I'll take that as a compliment." He plucked a strawberry from the plate on the dresser and bit into it.

"Excuse me. Didn't it occur to you I might have spent some time setting up that arrangement?"

"How could it not occur to me? I've watched you spend half an hour waiting for a sunbeam to fall just right."

"You have not."

"Close enough. But food is meant to be eaten, not stared at." He reached for another strawberry and held it temptingly close to her mouth.

She hesitated for the briefest moment before taking a bite. The combination of cool fruit and warm lips against his fingertips made him hot all over. He saw her shiver. Saw her throat work as she swallowed hard. She took a half step back—reluctantly, he would swear.

He vowed to close that gap again before they finished this conversation.

Her laugh sounded unsteady. "Good thing I didn't prep that plate for a real photo shoot."

"Why?"

"A professional food stylist might have sprayed everything with cornstarch and water to make it shine. Or brushed it with oil. Or even have used fake strawberries."

"Is that so? Well, you learn something every day."

"I'd like to learn a few things, too."

Maybe that explained why she had backed away. "Well, don't be shy," he murmured. The small line appearing between her eyebrows told him not to ask, but curiosity drove him to it. "Something wrong?"

"That was *my* question."

Her tone sounded cool and businesslike. He was still too hot to care.

"Have you got a problem with Rachel talking with me," she went on, "or is it me talking to Rachel that bothers you?"

"Neither."

"Then why do you cut us off whenever we say something to each other—or even try to?"

"I don't."

"You do." She smiled wryly. "I wish I'd had a tape

recorder handy so I could play every conversation back for you."

"Can't your fancy cameras handle that job?"

She shook her head in mock despair. "Do I bring out the worst in you? Or is this just as good as it gets?"

He looked down at the Stetson he'd removed upon entering the hotel and fiddled with the brim. She had a point—though he'd eat an entire supper of fake food before he'd admit it.

On the other hand, he could tell her the truth about why he wanted to keep her and Rachel apart. Or at least, part of the truth. "Look. You and Andi don't visit the ranch very often. Rachel barely knows you, but that wouldn't matter to her. She's got a tendency to latch on to folks very quickly."

"Some people might call that a knack for making friends. It's obvious you're not happy with the two of us having a conversation. Why not? After all, it isn't like I'm a complete stranger to you."

"As good as."

"After all these years?"

Her steady stare made his shoulders stiffen. He was botching this situation entirely, and they both knew it. He sure wouldn't own up to the biggest reason he didn't want her around his kids. But he had to do something to take that mistrustful look from her face.

"All right." He sighed. "I can't have you thinking I'm an ogre for not letting Rachel see her mama and a bastard for not being more accepting of my ex-wife." He turned to lean against the dresser and cross his arms over his chest. It kept him from having to look in her eyes. "What do you know about Marina's rise to fame?"

"She was an overnight sensation and she's doing extremely well."

"That about covers it," he said. "One day on a trip to Santa Fe, she was discovered in an outlet store by some talent scout who handed her his card. Maybe some women would have laughed it off or forgotten it."

"I don't know. That chance would be a hard one to miss."

"Marina didn't miss it. She jumped on it. She was always meant for something bigger and better than Cowboy Creek. Or so she kept telling me. When she left, Eric was only a couple of months old. Rachel was three. They both took her absence hard. Very hard."

"It must have been tough for you, too, being left with two babies." She rested her hand on his arm. "I may not know much about kids, Pete, but I can tell what a good father you are. I can see you're doing a wonderful job."

He still couldn't look her way, but the muscles in his shoulders unknotted. "Just trying to watch out for my kids."

"The way my father did with me."

Now he turned to look at her.

She smiled wryly. "Remember that first date you wanted me to tell you about?"

"When you were seventeen."

She nodded. "My dad chaperoned. A Christmas Ball at the officers' club."

"That must have put a damper on things."

"I managed." She raised her chin defiantly, but her cheeks turned pink.

The sight pleased him. She was such a mix of sophistication and shyness. "Let me guess. That's where you got your first kiss?" He'd figured the question would get to her, and it did.

Looking away, she ran her fingertips along the edge

of the dresser. "Yes. At the end of the dance. Only I had to make the first move."

"Are you kidding me?"

"Nobody messes with a general's daughter."

She laughed, and as always, the low, husky note drew him in, making him shift a half step nearer. Though her eyes widened, she didn't back off. Neither would he. He rested his hand on the dresser. His fingertips brushed hers.

"We'll see about that." He smiled. "Remember, I'm not shy. Why don't we find out the truth of that?"

"*Why* is the key word, cowboy."

A telltale twitch at the corner of her mouth said she held back a smile of her own. "Because," he said slowly, "there's something between us that *we* ought to put a damper on—before it gets out of hand."

"And a kiss is going to solve this?"

"Then you admit there's something there?"

"Maybe. But that doesn't mean we have to act on it."

Always good for an argument, this lady. Her defiant tone combined with the deepening pink of her cheeks only increased his need to kiss her. "Why not?" he murmured. "We could get it out of our systems. If you don't agree, then why don't you back away?"

"You first."

He laughed. She was playing him—just the way he was playing her. As if this were their first dance, set to words instead of music. Set to end the way her first dance had done? He shuffled another half step toward her, moving so close she had to look up to hold his gaze. "Honey, I'm not going anywhere."

"Neither am I."

He touched her face, his fingertips barely brushing her soft cheek. He ran his finger along her jawline. She didn't move, didn't protest, didn't say a word. A first for her, in his experience.

Her silent acceptance was as good as an invitation.

Chapter Seven

Pete's lips, warm and firm, tasted of strawberries. He pressed his mouth against hers and his hand against her back, as if he wanted more of her.

She wanted more of him, too. She touched his face with her fingertips, stroking the ridge of cheekbones, the scratch of late-day beard. Then she ran her hands through his hair, tugging him closer. If he meant for this kiss to put the damper on the attraction between them, she was darned sure going to enjoy the heat before the fire went out.

He kissed her long and hard and thoroughly, leaving her shaky enough to suspect New Mexico had been hit by an earthquake.

Then he eased up, turning his kiss soft and sweet. Sweet enough to make a woman lose herself in it.

She *would* have been lost, if not for the voice suddenly ringing in her head. Not the voice of reason, but the voice of his little girl. It wasn't until she heard the question repeated that she realized Rachel stood only a few feet away.

Jane took her hands from Pete's shoulders and forced herself not to think of what his daughter had just seen.

Later, in the privacy of her room, she would recall every lovely moment of every earth-moving touch. Now she had to act as if nothing much had happened. She only hoped she could rise to the challenge with Rachel standing in the bedroom doorway, both hands clapped over her mouth to hide her grin.

"What's that you're wearing, Rachel?" Pete's question sent out a warning note. Frowning, he looked his daughter over from head to toe.

"It's Jane's shirt. And Paz let me wear her necklaces—look." She lifted the cascading beaded ropes. "Red and blue and green and purple. I like the red one the best."

"Why don't you go visit with Paz in the kitchen?"

"But, Daddy, Jane's going to take my picture."

"Not today, sweetheart. Jane and I have to talk. You can show Paz and Tina and Andi how nice Paz's necklaces look."

She hesitated, her torn expression revealing she wanted to show off her borrowed clothes and jewelry as much as she wanted to protest. The idea of the fashion show won out, and she nodded happily. "Okay, I will."

The sound of her footsteps hadn't yet faded when Pete turned and said, "What's with the outfit?"

"I was going to give Rachel an idea of what a photo shoot is like. Just some fun for her."

He shook his head. "Don't encourage her."

"What's the problem with taking a few photos? You may never use the camera on your phone, but other people must have taken Rachel's picture in the past, probably many times. Aren't you overreacting?"

"Maybe I am." He shrugged, looked away, then looked back. "Maybe I've got reasons."

"Well—" Catching herself, she nodded. "All right. But just so you know, the photos wouldn't have been for the website. Even if I had planned to use them, I wouldn't publish anything without your permission, if that's your worry."

"You don't need to know all my worries."

She inhaled sharply and bit her lip to hold back her instinctive response. The sting of her teeth against her bottom lip, tender from his kisses, almost brought her to tears. Not of pain but of regret. How could he kiss her so gently and sweetly, then moments later brush off her concern?

His reaction to the innocent situation seemed out of proportion, to say the least. Still, she had no clue where his anger was coming from or what other situations he might have faced in the past. As he had said, maybe he had reasons. And as she had learned from Tina and Ally on Saturday, he was a very private man.

"I'm sorry. Information is easily spread and just as easily gathered—possibly by the wrong people. As a journalist I know that, and as a parent you have the right—and the obligation—to protect your kids."

"And I intend to." Though he was frowning just as he had when he'd questioned his daughter, his voice had calmed considerably, too. "It's not the photos. It's Rachel. She's already too wrapped up in herself. I'm trying to curb that, and your focus on her isn't helping."

"But this was no big deal. I was only going to take a few still shots. I thought Rachel—and you—would like the photos. She looks adorable."

"And like she's going to a funeral."

"Black's very fashionable."

"Pink's prettier on a little girl."

"Well...you may be right. But the color of the shirt doesn't matter, Pete. Rachel probably didn't even notice or care. She just wanted to pretend. All little girls like to play dress-up."

"You've had a lot of experience with kids?"

He had her there. "No. But I was a little girl once, too."

"And you're planning to have a few of your own someday?"

"Maybe..." Or maybe not. "When the right man comes along." *That* ought to give him something to think about.

He eyed her for a moment. "It's time for us to be getting home. Sharon will have supper ready. I'll make sure you get your shirt back. Rachel will have plenty of opportunities to shine at the wedding and at her graduation." He sighed. "Just do me a favor, and don't question how I raise my kids."

Before she could respond, he left the room.

He'd gotten the last word, but she hoped her remark about "the right man" had made an impression. At the very least, she hoped it proved to him he meant nothing to her. Their kiss meant nothing to her.

How could it, when it would never be repeated and she would soon go home?

She thought again of Rachel. Knowing Pete wouldn't trust her around his daughter left her heartsick.

He was right about her lack of experience with children. She had no skills when it came to kids. And her job left her no time to raise a family.

But he couldn't have known all that.

Why she wanted him to feel comfortable having her near his daughter, she really couldn't say—except, to her surprise, she had begun to develop a soft spot in her heart for the little girl. Obviously, she missed her mother. Just as obviously, she needed another little girl to play with.

Rachel and Robbie were so isolated here on the ranch, just the way she had felt as a child, moving from base to base, always having to make new friends.

Worse, she suspected Rachel shared things with her

she felt she couldn't tell anyone else, especially her daddy, who, when he talked with her, "just looked sad."

Maybe he didn't have all the answers about kids, either. Surprisingly, the thought revealed another soft spot in her heart.

She rested one hand on her camera and with the other poked at the remaining strawberries on the plate.

Pete had tasted like strawberries when he'd kissed her.

She had to admit, kissing him in real life had been even better than in her fantasies. As was the man himself. Now that she understood what made him so uptight about her being near his children, now that she'd seen that protectiveness in action, she could view him in a different light. She saw him as a loving daddy, a champion and guardian, and as an even more interesting man.

And as one heck of a kisser.

A fling with him could easily have provided a nice diversion until she left the ranch. But now that damper he'd wanted to put into place had well and truly slammed shut.

NO MATTER THE pleasure Pete had found in kissing Jane—and he *had* found it a pleasure—he'd confirmed that giving in to his attraction was one hell of a mistake.

He couldn't afford to make another one.

Already, he'd gone over the edge when he had found Rachel all dressed up for a photo shoot. He'd told Jane his reasons for not wanting his little girl to get that kind of extra attention, and still she'd pushed him.

He could explain everything, could tell her about Rachel missing her mama and his need to protect her from more disappointments. But Jane was here only for another week or so, not long enough for him to get comfortable spilling his guts, yet way too long for his peace of mind as far as Rachel's interest in her.

No, as he'd told Jane, she didn't need to know all his worries. And he'd do best to keep both those worries and his hands to himself.

Rachel's pouting on the way home didn't help the situation.

When they reached the front steps, she dug in her heels like a contrary mule. "I wanted Jane to take my picture."

"I know you did," he said.

"And Jane didn't ask me about helping me with the flowers. I said 'today?' and she said 'today or tomorrow,' remember, Daddy? But that was *last week*. And she *promised*."

He set his jaw. He'd figured the woman wouldn't follow through on that. More reason for him to keep his kids and himself away from her.

Sighing, he glanced at Rachel. They were on the verge of one of those long-delayed talks he needed to have with her. "I'm sorry, sweetheart, but that's the way life is. We don't always get what we want."

"Why?"

"Well—" he rubbed his chin "—sometimes, because the time isn't right."

"It was right today." She turned to him, her green eyes bright with tears. "I had Jane's shirt and Paz's necklaces for the picture. I was *all ready*!"

"Yes. I know you were." Even as her frustration sent his guilt soaring, it made him keep his voice deliberately level and low.

"Then why?"

"Because sometimes somebody else makes the rules."

You'll understand when you're older.

Useless to say that to her. It hadn't worked when his own father had tried it on him, had it? "Sweetheart, I know it's not easy to understand, but you can't always have things just the way you want them. Like when you're playing with Robbie."

"I share Bingo with him...sometimes."

"I know you do. I see you minding your manners more lately." *And not pestering Jane about broken promises.* He ruffled her wavy hair.

"I could share more," she admitted. Her eyes lit up. "When I practice with Jane and the flowers, I could let her have some to drop on the floor. That would be sharing, too, right?"

"Right." He didn't want to tell her the long odds of that happening or to have this talk focus on Jane. "Sharing can sometimes mean more than giving someone your toys. It means giving them a turn or listening to what they have to say. Like when you're with Robbie. Once in a while, you can let him choose the game or decide what you're going to play."

"But *my* ideas are better!"

It was all he could do not to laugh.

THE URGE TO laugh left Pete completely when he and Rachel entered the house and went into the kitchen. The sight of his father sitting at the table holding Eric on his knee made his day complete.

A complete disaster.

The kids were thrilled, but he just didn't need to deal with Mark right now. He had too many other things on his mind.

Quickly, he had excused himself. As he washed up and changed into fresh clothes, he made a point of looking into the mirror to make sure he wore a civil expression.

He'd told Jane he could keep his feelings to himself. That included when he was around his father. He and the man couldn't agree on a viewpoint if they were both looking through a pair of binoculars together. Still, he had to admit Mark never let his feelings about his son affect his relationship with his grandkids.

He returned to the kitchen to find Mark protesting the idea of staying for supper.

"No, no, I wouldn't put you out at the last minute like this."

"It's not putting us out a bit," Sharon said. "Stew can always stretch to feed one more. And I've already added extra noodles to the pot."

Fortunately, his father accepted.

Fortunately, because otherwise, who knew when they would see him again. He might be a good grandfather, but he wasn't often a visitor. A couple of years ago, Pete had to suggest Rachel call his father "Grandpa Mark," as the kids were much more familiar with "Grandpa Jed."

With some help from Rachel, he and Sharon got supper on the table, while Mark settled Eric in the high chair.

Sharing a meal with his father didn't top his list of favorite things to do. Ironically, that thought only reminded him of what he'd told Rachel. *We don't always get what we want.* But for his kids' sake, he'd make it through this.

"More stew, Mark?" Sharon asked.

Not exactly the cuisine the man was used to, but he accepted the bowl when Sharon passed it his way.

"I helped peel the carrots," Rachel told Mark.

"Did you?" he asked. "That's good training for you."

"Rachel's always a big help to me," Sharon told him. "She's a very good worker."

"And you do a great job, Rachel," he said. "It sounds like Sharon picked just the right job for you."

"Yeah," Rachel said happily.

Pete ignored the jab at him, a reminder of the never-ending arguments he had gotten from his father once he'd taken the wrangler position here at Garland Ranch. Mark was definitely of the belief that the sooner kids were put to work, the better—provided that work met with his approval.

Pushing the thoughts aside, he made an attempt to act civil. "So, what brings you down our way?"

"Just one item in a busy week. I'm en route to Santa Fe again after a meeting in Otero County. Tomorrow, I'm flying to Washington for a couple of days to speak before a Senate committee. Then I'll be off to Albany for a special meeting of the New York State Bar Association." Quite a list, but Pete had heard longer, and so had his kids. "Never a dull moment."

"I'll bet."

Unlike your life, his father's quick smile seemed to say.

Pete would have shoved aside his interpretation as a bad case of paranoia, except that the man had used exactly those words with him more than once. Mark Brannigan might be the smoothest-talking attorney in the state of New Mexico, but he didn't mind turning rough when he talked to his son.

His father was disappointed in him for not living up to his expectations. For not carrying on the family tradition and adding another Brannigan to the law firm's letterhead. Pete got that. That didn't mean he cared. He hadn't been kidding when he'd asked Jane what was wrong with old-fashioned cowboy values. He only hoped he would show more understanding and be less demanding of his own kids when they grew up.

"Grandpa Mark, you're always busy, aren't you?" Rachel asked.

He smiled at her. "I am. But it keeps me out of trouble."

Her eyes rounded. "Grown-ups get in trouble, too?"

"They sure do."

"Is kissing somebody trouble?"

"*Kissing?* At your age, Rachel? I think your father would have something to say about that."

"Not *me*!" Giggling, she shot a glance toward Pete.

"You planning to be in the state between now and the end of the month?" He asked the question quickly in case Rachel decided to share what she'd seen in the hotel suite.

Eric banged on his high-chair tray, scattering pieces of the biscuit he'd crumbled to bits.

A few of those crumbs landed on the long sleeve of Mark's starched white shirt. He brushed them onto his napkin and went on with his to-do list. "No. The rest of the month is just as busy, ending with an address to the UNM School of Law's seniors prior to their graduation."

"Graduation!" Rachel exclaimed. "I forgot. Grandpa Mark, I have to give you the invitation for my graduation."

"And when is that?"

"It's…" She looked at Pete, who supplied the date.

"I won't be able to make it—"

"But you *have* to."

"As much as I would like that, Rachel, I'm afraid I can't. But I'll stop by again and take you for a treat the next time I'm able, all right?"

Rachel eyed him for a long moment, then shrugged.

She'd managed to brush off the disappointment the way Mark had brushed biscuit crumbs from his sleeve. If only she could as easily deal with missing her mother. If only he could find the right way to help her.

"Okay. I'll give your invitation to Sugar."

"Sugar?"

From long years of being on the receiving end of it, Pete recognized his father's method of "clarifying a statement without leading the witness." Before moving his law practice to Santa Fe, Mark had lived his entire life in Cowboy Creek. He knew the name of the local bakery owner.

"Yes, Sugar," Rachel confirmed. "From SugarPie's."

"Well, I admire *your* resourcefulness and flexibility, Rachel."

A silence followed, in which Pete wished he could blame paranoia for his interpretation of his father's emphasis.

The sound of the doorbell ringing startled Eric. His hands jerked, spraying biscuit crumbs in all directions.

"I'll get it." Pete rose, happy for the break from Mark's pointed comments.

WHEN PETE SAW Jane standing on the doorstep, his happiness crumbled like the biscuit on Eric's tray. Stepping onto the porch, he pulled the door half-closed behind him.

His memory conjured up an image of his last encounter with her, of the way they'd played each other and where that had led them. To an action he had thought about more than a dozen times since he'd left her in that hotel room. An action he couldn't think about repeating. Yet when his gaze homed in on her mouth and she pressed her soft, sweet lips together, he couldn't help his rush of satisfaction at the certainty she was remembering their kiss, too.

Or was she?

He recalled how easily she'd managed to move away from him when Rachel had appeared on the scene.

Then he thought of the half-opened door behind him. Of his family just a few rooms away. Of Rachel's giggle at the supper table and earlier, when she had found them in the hotel suite. The images were enough—just barely enough—to prevent him from touching Jane.

But they couldn't stop him from playing the role he automatically assumed when he was with her. "You back for more?"

"More?"

"Of what we left half-finished."

"I thought we *had* finished. We took care of things before they got out of hand. Got it out of our systems. Remember?" Her smile didn't reach her eyes. "Actually, I've come to see Rachel. When she was over at the hotel earlier, I told her I'd play a game with her."

"So, that's one promise you're keeping?"

"Excuse me?"

"What happened with the flowers?"

"Oh…" She winced. "I forgot."

"Right," he said flatly.

She sighed. "Pete, that didn't have to be done today. We still have plenty of time before the wedding."

"Time works in funny ways when you're five years old."

"So I hear." Now her eyes gleamed.

"And she heard you say you'd help her with the flowers last week. Five-year-olds have long memories." He shook his head. "Forget it. Anyway, we're still at supper. And she didn't mention anything about a game. Just as well, since—"

The door swung open behind him. Rachel appeared at his elbow. "Jane! Do you want to take my picture now?"

She shook her head. "I didn't bring my cameras."

"Oh…well, that's okay." Rachel took her by the hand. "Come and see my grandpa Mark. He's in the kitchen."

As they entered the house, Pete followed. He would rather go down the porch steps and keep walking, maybe to the coolness and quietness of the barn. He felt grounded there. Sane. Not the way he did when he was around Jane and couldn't make up his mind which way he wanted to go.

But he couldn't leave Sharon to deal with everyone.

Jane didn't need anyone's help. She could stand up to his father.

On his way back to the kitchen, he spent most of the time guessing which of the two would throw out the first barbed remark. A much-needed diversion—because otherwise, despite his irritation, he'd obsess over how he could get her alone.

Chapter Eight

So much for worrying about the meeting between his father and Jane. Mark had taken to her as readily as if she were his long-lost daughter. As quickly as his kids had taken a shine to her. And, if he would admit the truth, as easily as he had given in to his attraction today.

His father directed most of his comments to Jane. Rachel sat fidgeting with her slice of apple pie. He could see the repeated efforts she made not to interrupt—not that she would have had much chance. Eric played with a couple of cookies. He and Sharon followed the kids' leads and focused on their desserts.

Jane's glamorous, globe-trotting career had a lot to do with his father's interest. Mark had given Marina's modeling career a nod of approval, but he seemed to have awarded Jane's job a much higher ranking.

"A genuine challenge." Mark gave a self-deprecating laugh. "Not unlike the practice of law. While I attempt to find the truth in a courtroom, you search for it all over the world."

"Any kind of work can be challenging if it interests you," Pete put in.

"True," Jane said.

She gave him a smile that would've left his knees shaking if he'd been standing. Was she coming on to him right here? Or was she, like Mark, simply turning on the sophisticated charm?

"I've interviewed so many subjects whose jobs most people wouldn't think twice about," she went on, "yet once you get them talking, once you dig beneath the surface, they have some fascinating stories to tell."

"Jane takes lots of pictures," Rachel said. "Of the hotel and places and people. She showed them to me."

Jane met his eyes. "The less controversial ones," she murmured.

The added draw of her five-star-general father hadn't hurt her ratings with Mark. But it was learning she had photographed some of the biggest names in Washington that really won him over.

As much as Jed bragged about this granddaughter of his, he had never mentioned her political connections. The news made an impression on Pete now, too, but not for the better. It reinforced the similarities between her and his ex. She moved in the same kind of crowd his ex-wife did. And like Marina, she would never settle for being a small-town girl and a ranch manager's wife.

His father dropped a few high-powered names of his own. "I'd like to see some of those photographs Rachel mentioned."

"They're on my computer over at the hotel," she told him.

"Well, then." Mark pushed his plate away from him, the slice of pie on it barely touched. "We'll have to go find your computer. I've already seen some of your magazine work, of course. Very impressive."

"Thank you."

"I can see where it would hold an interest for collectors. Have you ever thought of offering some of your private photos for sale?"

"Yes, I have. I just haven't had time to put a decent portfolio together. And I'd need to find a gallery interested in photography and, of course, in what I'd plan to show."

"I might be able to assist you there," Mark said. "I have some connections to the art world. Why don't we see what you've got?"

"Thanks, I'd love that. But you don't need to think about it right now." She glanced around the table. Her gaze met Pete's for the briefest moment, then moved on to Rachel and Eric. "I wouldn't want to take you away from your family."

"That's not an issue. I was getting ready to leave when you arrived." Mark stood and reached across the table. "Pete, it's been good seeing you and the kids. Sharon, a pleasure, as always."

"Do you have to leave, Grandpa Mark?" Rachel asked.

"Yes, I'm afraid I do."

He kissed both kids.

When he began to escort Jane from the room, he was already deep in conversation with her again.

Jane waved a quick goodbye but didn't stop to chat, didn't glance back and apparently didn't give Rachel another thought.

Still at the table, Pete sat with his hand clamped on the edge of his dessert plate as he watched his daughter. Disappointment showed clearly in her face.

"Jane forgot her cameras for my picture," she said in a low voice. Strike one against the woman. He watched Rachel stare down at her plate. "I just said okay, Daddy. Because you told me I can't always have what I want."

"Yes, I did tell you that."

"And Jane forgot we were gonna play a game because she went with Grandpa Mark." Strike two, as far as he was concerned. "But that's okay, too." She looked up at him. "Because that's how I can share Jane, right?"

"Right." He coughed, then tried again. "That's right, sweetheart. I'm very proud of you."

Over her head, he met Sharon's gaze.

"Rachel," Sharon said, "will you take this to the sink?" She handed over the metal bowl she had used to serve the biscuits.

As the two of them set to work, Pete turned to clean off Eric's tray and tried to get a handle on his thoughts.

Being a daddy had always been challenging. But his job got more complicated by the minute, thanks to Marina and Mark. And now Jane.

His interest in her gave way to irritation on his daughter's behalf. He didn't want Jane around his family anyhow. Why should he care that she'd walked off without another word?

Easy answer, he reassured himself, after another quick look at Rachel. He'd hate seeing *anyone* break a promise to one of his kids.

JED ENTERED THE office behind the registration desk, where Tina did most of her bookkeeping, along with keeping track of the construction work going on around the hotel. "What are you doing in here so late? Shouldn't you be spending the evening with your intended?"

"I will be. And with you and Andi and Jane and everybody else. I just wanted to get the checks ready for the contractors for the next phase of the renovations."

"Good. But speaking of Jane, have you seen her lately?"

"Mmm... I may have caught a glimpse of her going out onto the front porch with Pete's dad just a minute ago." She smiled. "Abuelo, I've had my eye on you, and I have a feeling you're up to something."

"Why should you think that? Can't I ask the whereabouts of one of my own granddaughters without having a reason?"

"Says the man who got me this." She held out her left hand and wiggled her fingers, making her diamond engagement ring sparkle in the light from the desk lamp.

He laughed. "Well, I reckon Cole had some part in that, too."

"Oh, so you admit you can't do everything all alone?"

"I'll admit nothing of the sort." He leaned forward and lowered his voice. "But what have you got in mind?"

"Not a thing. I just wanted to advise you, in case you're trying to play matchmaker with Jane and Pete, you're going to have your hands full."

"Don't I know it. They're both a couple of tough nuts to crack."

"Well, don't worry. I *have* seen a few signs of splintering in Jane—and Cole mentioned Pete's been very distracted. But you didn't hear either of those from me."

"As if I'd turn around and tell one of 'em? You know me better than that."

She laughed.

He grinned back at her. "That's my girl. You see or hear anything else, you be sure to let me know. I can handle anything, but it never hurts to have a backup."

At the sound of a discreet buzz, a sign the front door had just been opened, they both turned toward the office doorway. "I reckon that's her on her way back in. My turn now," he murmured, winking.

When they saw Jane pass by in the lobby, Tina rose from her seat and called her name. "Good luck," Tina murmured to Jed.

She left the room, and he heard her say, "Grandpa's looking for you."

A moment later, Jane appeared in the doorway. "What's up?"

"I heard Mark Brannigan had stopped in—not that I'm overly curious about the matter. But it surprised me he didn't drop by to say hello."

Jane swallowed a smile. In her experience, Jed had always been curious about everything, and he'd never been backward about asking whatever he wanted to know. He was fishing for information.

Right now, so was she.

She took the seat behind Tina's desk. "I'd gone over to see Rachel, and he was there for dinner." Briefly, she explained what had led to Mark's visit to the Hitching Post.

"He's got a lot of influence here," he told her. "It would be nice if he worked something out for you with the photos."

She might have just as much luck going through her contacts in New York, but there was no need to say that. "He had to get back to Santa Fe. He sent his regards and said he would see you next time."

"That's one busy man."

"Yes. He was telling me about his legal work and other commitments. It sounds like he doesn't have much time for himself."

"Sad, isn't it?"

"His accomplishments are impressive, though."

"That's all well and good, and I respect the man for it. But life's not all about working, especially when it keeps him from seeing his family." The innocent look in his bright blue eyes would have had a panhandler offering *him* cash.

She knew where he was headed with this conversation—into a topic she wanted to avoid. Changing the subject landed her in another area she hadn't intended to explore. Much. "There seems to be some…tension between Mark and Pete."

"Mark never did care for his son's choice of career," he said promptly. "Wanted him to take his place in the family firm."

"Become a lawyer? Pete would hate that."

"Right you are." He chuckled. "Sounds like you know the man better than his own daddy does."

She rested her elbows on the desk and leaned forward, half hoping the desk lamp would account for the heat filling her face. "I don't know him at all, Grandpa."

Then why had she been kissing the man?

And why was she thinking about that now?

"It wasn't Pete I wanted to talk about, but Rachel. You were right. She's gotten very attached to me."

"Yep. I could see that when you were here on your last visit."

She stared. "That was a couple of months ago."

"And it's been going on longer than that."

"But…it had been a while since my trip before that. That time, I didn't even see her. I'm sure of it."

"I'm not talking about the girl's attachment to you specifically. I mean the fact she's looking for her mama."

"I'm not—" She blinked to clear her suddenly blurry vision. "I don't look at all like Marina. And Rachel knows her mother has blond hair. She told me that herself."

"She hasn't seen her for so long, I'd reckon it's about all she knows."

"That's awful." Her voice broke.

He shrugged. Deepening frown lines had dimmed the sparkle in his eyes, too. "I know it is, girl. Last time Marina visited, Eric was just a year old, Rachel still a baby herself. Who can tell just what the child remembers?"

When Jane rang the doorbell of Pete's house a second time that evening, it took longer than before for him to come to the door. His reaction to seeing her hadn't changed, though. Again, after their eyes met, his gaze drifted to her mouth, and once again, her heart gave a senseless, erratic thump.

Unexpectedly, he stepped out onto the porch. He stood so close, his shirtfront almost brushed hers. Casually, she hoped, she took a half step backward.

"I came to see Rachel," she explained.

"It's too late," he said flatly. "She's in bed."

"Already?"

"She's five. And she's got school tomorrow."

"Oh, right. Of course."

Why did she feel so darned edgy standing here with him?

She gave herself a mental shake. Pete couldn't possibly read anything into her visit—not after their previous conversation here on this porch. She had no reason to feel uneasy. The glow from the porch fixture throwing a harsh light on his face couldn't be any more flattering to hers. That didn't matter. She hadn't planned to seduce him. The kiss they shared that afternoon was becoming a precious but distant memory. Just as well. They weren't lovers, only two people who had nothing much in common but their concern for his children.

The thought of his love for the kids worked to calm her down. Much more casually now, she stepped aside. She should go. But she felt the need to stay for Rachel's sake. And Pete's.

He hadn't moved.

"Sorry," she said. "I should have realized it was too late for Rachel to be up. Tina and Andi have already tucked their kids in for the night, too. I meant to come back sooner, but your dad and I got wrapped up in our conversation. And my photos." She smiled. "He's going to talk to a couple of gallery owners he knows, one in Santa Fe and another in San Antonio. It's very nice of him to take the time and make the effort."

"Yeah. Nice."

She tried not to frown. Pete's steady stare and even more level tone were bringing her nerves to a head again. The reaction wasn't like her and was ridiculous, besides. She crossed her arms and settled more firmly against the railing.

"No matter what comes of his offer, I owe him a big thanks. Our conversation made me realize that, between assignments and deadlines and travel for the job, I haven't paid as much attention to my own photography as I should. And that I need to *make* the time to get my work ready to show.

"I've got contacts, too, all over the world, especially in New York." Now she was babbling. Judging by Pete's frozen expression, none of this was of interest to him.

"Anyhow, I'll follow up with Rachel tomorrow. After that, things will get hectic at the hotel, with Andi's father arriving tomorrow night and my parents flying in on Friday. And then there's all the prepping for the wedding. In fact, I should go back and talk with Paz and Tina now about the game plan."

His lack of response rattled her, yet knowing how much he cared about his daughter, she pushed on. She had to share her thoughts about Rachel. "As long as we're out here…" Still, he said nothing. She took a deep breath. "I understand your concerns about Rachel, and I don't want to interfere. But I think there's something you should know."

He edged a step closer and crossed his arms over his

chest. Again, she thought of the glare from the porch fixture on her face, which now made her feel exposed. She could see—and couldn't help but admire—the bulge of muscle beneath his T-shirt sleeves. But she didn't like that the movement left him with his back to the light, hiding his expression in the shadows.

She wondered if he'd shifted for just that reason.

"You were saying…?" he prompted.

"What?"

"There's something I needed to know."

"Yes. I know you told me about Marina leaving the kids, and I realize I've been here only for a few days this time around. But I've spent some time with Rachel, and she played with Robbie and Trey over at the hotel most of yesterday afternoon." She took another deep breath. "From what I've seen and things she has said, I think she misses her mother very much."

Pete's shoulders went back. Instead of simply putting space between them, the movement seemed to make him taller and broader. And menacing.

She shook her head, both to deny the feeling and to shake some sense into herself. These reactions were completely unlike her, and falling apart wouldn't do a thing to add to her credibility. "I know your wife—"

"Ex-wife."

"—ex-wife hasn't been back to Cowboy Creek for a while, and I've come up with an idea that might bring her around. Grandpa's determined to make the Hitching Post a destination-wedding locale, and in order to do that, we could use a hook. A draw. A name and face to put on the website." The more she talked about her brainstorm, the more excited she became. "Marina, as a local-girl-turned-celebrity, would be perfect as the spokesperson for the hotel. And at the same time, she could—"

"Forget it."

"But she—"

"It won't work."

She frowned. "How can you say that when you haven't heard the rest of my idea yet?"

"I don't need to hear it. It won't work."

"Because you're determined not to let it work."

"It's got nothing to do with me."

It's got everything *to do with you.*

"Look," he continued, "you don't know anything about my history with my ex, only the small part I told you about her leaving. As for following up with Rachel—don't. She wasn't happy after you walked off with my father, when you had promised to play a game with her. And she doesn't need any more broken promises."

The unfairness of his accusation left her speechless. She hadn't broken her promise to his daughter; she had just run into a temporary distraction. Finally, she said, "I *did* come back."

"Yeah." He nodded. "As I just said, it's too late."

He murmured a good-night and returned to the house.

Chapter Nine

Late the next afternoon, Jane finally managed to get Tina alone in her office behind the registration desk.

"I'm back—as if that's not obvious," she told Tina with a laugh. "I brought Robbie home with me, too."

Earlier, she had made sure she was near the lobby when the school bus arrived. Rachel had seemed ecstatic that Jane had remembered her promise about their game.

Together with Robbie, they had walked the short distance to Pete's house, where Sharon had welcomed them all into the kitchen.

Eric had taken a nap, and Sharon had ironed laundry, leaving the three of them to play Rachel's choice of games at the kitchen table. One round of the board game had led to three more. When they were done, Rachel's efforts to convince her to stay had only reinforced Jane's thoughts about Pete's little girl.

Jane had no doubt Sharon was a wonderful housekeeper and babysitter. But after giving her conversation with Jed some thought, she decided he had been right. Obviously, Rachel was looking for someone closer to her mother's age to cling to, trying to find a replacement for the parent she no longer had.

"How did the games go?" Tina asked.

"Well…let's just say Rachel has a well-developed competitive streak."

"And Robbie's isn't bad, either, is it? You don't need to hide that from me."

"I was more concerned about not letting you know I'm fairly competitive myself."

Tina laughed, but a small, vertical line appeared above her eyes as she looked at the file folder in front of her on the desk. With a sigh, she closed the folder and pushed it aside.

"Better stop frowning," Jane advised, "or those lines in your forehead will have to be edited out of the wedding photos."

Tina shook her head. "I'm beginning to believe I'll have permanent frown lines from now on. It's these contractors." She sighed again. "Of course, I've resigned myself to the fact our rooms won't be ready for a while yet." Tina and Cole were converting the hotel's spacious attic into an apartment for themselves and Robbie. "But I'd hoped they would have more of the guest rooms refurbished by now."

"At least the chapel and the banquet hall are ready for Saturday. I'm sorry you've had to deal with most of the headaches alone."

"Don't even think about that. Between Cole and Grandpa and Abuela, I have plenty of support. It's just, as Cole always says, I take everything more seriously than I should. We *have* made a lot of progress in only a couple of months."

Jane sat in the chair beside Tina's desk and picked up a plastic cube filled with colored paper clips. "I've had an idea for the hotel—and don't worry, it won't require any more renovations. Since you're more involved than any of us with the revamp, I wanted to run it by you first."

She also wanted more information and believed Tina was the best person to provide it. "I'm sure Grandpa will go for it, though." She outlined her plan to feature Pete's ex-wife on the hotel's website. "What do you think?"

"I think Grandpa would love the idea of a spokesperson for the Hitching Post."

"But…? I can hear it in your voice."

"But I'm not so sure how well Pete will like the idea of asking Marina."

"Not well at all." She rattled the container of paper clips. With a sigh of her own, she added, "Trust me on that."

"You've talked to him about it already?"

She nodded. "But he doesn't own the hotel. Grandpa wouldn't give him a say in it, would he?"

"I don't know… He's very close to Pete. He treats him just like family. We all do."

"Then you all must feel the same way about Pete's kids. Tina, I don't know if you've ever noticed or if Rachel has ever talked to you, but she really misses her mother."

"I know she does. But I don't know what we can do. As Ally and I said the other day, Pete's such a private person. He's never talked about why Marina hasn't come back for so long to see the kids. It's a sticky situation."

"Maybe he's made it that way."

"It could be," Tina admitted. "She didn't visit on a regular basis even before their divorce." Her dark eyes shone. "Considering the way my parents left me for Abuela to raise, I don't like to think of anyone abandoning their kids."

Which was virtually what Marina had done—to his children *and* to Pete. The thought made her breath catch. Was that why he blew up whenever he thought of her forgetting a promise to his daughter? Did he equate what he saw as her broken promises to his wife's broken wedding vows?

Tina sighed. "I can't believe—or maybe I don't want to believe—Pete's deliberately keeping Marina from the kids."

She didn't have quite the trouble Tina had with that scenario. Not meeting her cousin's eyes, she set the paper-clip dispenser on the desk. "Then you think it's his ex-wife's choice?"

"I don't have an answer for that, either. I don't know Marina that well. She was a few years ahead of me in school, a senior when I was a freshman, and our paths didn't cross that often. Ally's right, though—Marina does like to be in the limelight. Modeling's a perfect career for her. But from what I could tell whenever she was around, she's not a bad person at all. She's just…well, sort of like you, Jane. Not meant for life in a small town."

The statement made her pause. Why, when she had already acknowledged that herself? She took a deep breath. "I still think this is a good idea. Having Marina as spokesperson can serve multiple purposes. It will help Grandpa by increasing exposure for the wedding business and for the hotel in general. And it will give Pete's kids a chance to see their mother."

Tina nodded. "I think it's worth looking into whether or not she'd be interested."

"I do, too."

Pete would probably never speak to her again. But any dismay she felt at the thought was swept aside by the memory of yesterday's conversation with Rachel and the little girl's heartbreaking statement.

I think Mama forgot all about us.

Someone had to show Rachel that wasn't true.

And surely, if he had seen his daughter's tears, Pete would agree.

PETE STARED INTO his half-filled glass on the bar at the Cantina, Cowboy Creek's only combination restaurant and saloon. Instead of the dark gold of his beer, he was envisioning something in black.

Jane in black—because of course that was what she'd have on. She wore the damn color like a uniform, like her dad, the general. But Jane in a low-cut, tight-fitting dress…now, that would be something to see. And he *had* seen her dressed that way. In his dreams.

"Hey, Pete, what's going on?"

The groom-to-be clapped him on the shoulder. "I thought this was a bachelor party, not a funeral."

He tried not to wince as Cole's last word called to mind what he'd said about Rachel wearing Jane's shirt. Forcing a grin, he said, "I'm partying. I'm just sitting here rehearsing my next toast."

Cole laughed and took the bar stool next to his. "Forget it. Toasting time is over for tonight. We've lost the boys already."

A number of men from Cowboy Creek had shown up tonight by Pete's invitation. The one Cole would have chosen for his best man, Mitch Weston, couldn't make it. "A shame Mitch couldn't come home for the wedding."

The groom nodded. "He's too busy serving and protecting the folks of LA. Following in his father's footsteps." Mitch's dad was county sheriff in Cowboy Creek. "Unlike some of us."

After hearing about Mark's unhappiness over Pete's career, Cole had assured Pete he'd have made the same choice.

"Anyhow," Cole went on, "half the boys are out on the dance floor and the other half are evenly distributed between the dartboard and the pool table."

"Including your buddies?" Cole had asked two of his wrangler friends from Texas to make up the wedding party.

"My buddies." Cole snorted. "Oh, no, they've got other things on their minds. Your fellow usher's chatting up one of the waitresses over in the corner, and Tyler—" the best man "—has taken over the other corner with Shay from the Big Dipper. Not a bad thing, though, if he can sweet-talk her into a discount on ice cream."

Pete shook his head. "Guess you might as well have invited Tina to keep you company."

"And Jane to help set *your* mind at ease?"

"What does that mean?" he snapped.

"Whoa. No disrespect, boss—and remember, you can't take a swing at the groom. But—" Pete raised his glass "—though I've had a couple, it's not affecting my eyesight yet. Something's been worrying you this week, and it looks like you brought it along with you tonight."

He'd be damned if he would admit Jane had caused his distraction.

He hadn't seen her since their conversation on the porch Monday night. Her parents weren't due in until tomorrow, but according to Cole, Andi's dad had already arrived. He had thought he'd be grateful Jane's uncle provided a diversion for her, letting him off the hook about following her around the Hitching Post. The reality was, he kept coming up with crazy reasons to wander over to the hotel.

He shifted his beer glass on the bar. Then, glancing at Cole, he gave a response that covered part of the truth. "Rachel's been acting up."

"Ah," Cole said heavily, shaking his head. "Kids'll do that."

He grinned. "Listen to you, an expert already."

Cole, who had learned only a few months back that Robbie was his son, accepted the good-natured jab. "It feels that way sometimes," he bragged. "I wouldn't have it any other way. But I'm more skilled with boys than girls. And of course, I've always got Tina there to help me. I'd imagine that makes a difference."

"Yeah." He and Cole often talked about his single-dad status, but this was the closest his friend had ever come to making a comment about Marina.

Cole picked at the label on his bottle. "You sure it's Rachel that's worrying you this week, and not Jane? If so, maybe Tina could help you out, seeing as they're cousins."

"What does Jane have to do with anything?"

"I don't know. Maybe it was the way you snapped when I said her name. All I know is, when I came back to town, I got defensive whenever my sister mentioned Tina. The it-doesn't-matter kind of defensive. Probably why I recognize it in you now." He took a swig from the bottle. "But if it's really the kids you're needing some advice about, run things by Jed. He's a man in a million."

"He is that."

"Just be prepared. You'll soon find him encouraging you in a certain direction, nudging you toward the way he wants you to go."

"You sure you haven't gone over your limit on the beer? What are you talking about?" He had the sinking feeling he already knew. Should already have realized long before this.

Jed wasn't the kind of man to force someone to repay a debt. He wasn't the sort to keep reminding a man who owed him. But just like Pete, he darn sure was a man who would do anything for his family.

"Jed felt he knew what was best for me and Tina," Cole said.

"You mean he fixed you two up?"

"He was more devious than that, but yeah. He thought we were a pair. So I speak from experience when I tell you he thinks he knows what's best." Cole laughed. "And seeing how things turned out for me, I'd say he's right on the mark."

The idea of the boss giving his blessing to a relationship between his ranch manager and one of his granddaughters made Pete take a good, long swallow of beer to ease his tight throat. There was no one he respected more than Jed Garland. No one.

But this time the man had made a bad call.

Sure, Jane was getting better looking to him by the day. That kiss of theirs had left him wanting more. He'd envisioned having her in his bed. But his dreams about her had to stop there.

It would be safer for his kids if he didn't get attached to her.

He took another drink of his brew.

What was he thinking?

He'd never had plans to get attached to Jane. One kiss sure didn't mean they were joined at the hip. He wasn't connected emotionally or physically…only by a debt to her grandfather he could never fully repay.

Well, she would be busy with her parents flying in tomorrow and staying for the wedding. He would just avoid her for the rest of her visit. And once she had left, he'd stop thinking about her altogether.

He only prayed that Rachel would be more successful at that than he would.

"Sorry to tell you this, Cole." He forced himself to shake his head in sympathy. "If Jed thinks he's got another groom lined up for a second granddaughter, he's facing some real disappointment."

Chapter Ten

Twenty-four hours after the bachelor party, Pete sat in the dining room of the Hitching Post with another drink in front of him—this time, a glass of champagne. He'd needed something to cut the dryness in his throat.

In the small wedding chapel adjacent to the hotel, Father Alfredo and the wedding party had done a practice run-through for tomorrow's ceremony.

Just a couple of hours ago, he had learned he'd been paired with Jane. He'd had to take her by the arm to escort her down the aisle. Had to shorten his stride—though not by much—to match hers. Had to inhale the perfume she wore, the same vanilla and spice that had surprised him the first time he'd seen her in the barn.

He glanced toward the far side of the room, where she stood focusing her camera on the center table. Instead of the body-hugging dress of his dreams, she wore a long-sleeved black top and pants of some shimmery material. Every time she moved, the fabric sparkled like the skim of ice on a lake.

The thought of what Cole had told him about Jed's hopes for his eldest granddaughter had him wanting to shake his head. His interest in Jane hadn't eased one bit, but…anticipating a serious relationship with her? Not in this lifetime.

The dining room was crowded. Between the bride and groom, Jed and Paz, Jed's two sons and one daughter-in-law, and Father Alfredo, the main table was filled. The rest of the group had overflowed to some of the smaller ones set around the room.

Pete shared his table with Rachel and Jane. He wondered who'd come up with that seating arrangement.

At the center table, Cole's best man rose, champagne glass in hand. "I'd say these pre-wedding festivities call for a pre-wedding toast."

"You didn't do enough of that last night, Ty?" Cole asked, grinning.

"I'm practicing for tomorrow." Tyler raised his glass. "To the bride- and groom-to-be."

"Daddy, I can do the toast, too." Rachel grinned as widely as Cole had as she held up her long-stemmed glass filled with apple juice.

Jane's champagne sat untouched beside her empty plate. She hadn't eaten anything yet. In fact, she hadn't come near their table. All night, she had done nothing but prowl the room restlessly, her camera never out of her hands.

Pete focused on Rachel. As he smiled and touched his glass to hers, he thought again of what he'd said to Cole last night about facing disappointment. This time, he didn't think of Jed, who sat smiling from his seat at the head of the center table, but of Rachel and Eric. And, much as he didn't want to admit the truth, he thought of himself.

After his ex-wife had left to start her career, she'd come back from time to time to see the kids. But the space between those visits had lengthened with each one, until last year, when the divorce had become final. Since then, she hadn't been back once.

He knew Marina's hit-or-miss schedule upset both his children, especially Rachel. She was old enough to remember her mama's sudden appearances and disappearances, smart enough to notice how long it had been since they had seen Marina at all, and vulnerable enough to hang her heart on every single one of Marina's promises to visit. Promises she had broken, time after time.

Probably why he'd reacted so badly at hearing Jane make a promise to Rachel she hadn't fulfilled.

His ex-wife's interactions with the kids, like her visits before the divorce, had been superficial and fleeting. He could foresee the same situation developing with Jane. He couldn't fault her for that. But he could envision the impending disaster.

Like a newborn calf turning instinctively to seek its mama, Rachel had gravitated to Jane. Somehow Eric, young as he was, and maybe picking up on Rachel's actions, had done the same. Whether or not Jane realized or wanted or intended it, she was bonding with his kids. And just like with their mama, when Jane left, Rachel would be devastated.

"Daddy, doesn't Jane look so pretty?"

He froze, feeling sure everyone in the room had heard Rachel's question and sat waiting for his answer. To his surprise, when he glanced around, no one seemed to be paying him any attention.

"All the ladies look pretty tonight," he told Rachel. "Including my little lady."

She giggled. "You mean *me*!"

"I sure do."

She looked down at her white blouse and plucked at her red skirt. "This is okay, but not like my dress for tomorrow."

"I can hardly wait to see you in it," he assured her. And

he meant it. She had told him everything she could recall about the trips to the bridal shop in Santa Fe, everything except a description of the dresses, which had been kept top secret. And Rachel, chatterbox that she was, hadn't said a word. He was heart-bustingly proud of her.

His gaze went to Jane again, and he realized how eagerly he was waiting to see her dress for the wedding, too.

Looking at her brought on another bout of confusion.

He refused to think of his feelings about her. Yet, he'd continued to come up with excuses that would bring him near her. He didn't know how much longer he could fight them. Tonight, he felt damned grateful the decision had been taken out of his hands.

"Daddy, here comes Jane. She can take my picture now."

Jane must have overheard the statement. When she reached their table, she picked up her champagne glass without meeting his eyes.

"Do the toast with me," Rachel demanded.

Smiling, Jane touched glasses with her.

"Now do the toast with Daddy."

Her smile unwavering, Jane turned to him.

As they clicked their glasses together, the backs of their fingers brushed, just long enough for him to feel the heat of her skin.

"Can Jane take the picture now, Daddy?"

Jane's gaze met his. He nodded. She raised her glass slightly as if toasting him for agreeing, then took a sip of champagne.

Rachel settled herself in her chair, folded her hands in her lap and said, "I'm ready."

"Okay." Jane raised her camera. "Give me a big smile. That's it." The camera clicked. "All done."

Rachel slid from her seat. “I’m going to go talk to Robbie now.” A second later she was gone.

Frowning, Pete looked at Jane, who stood holding the camera in both hands. “That was quick.”

“Yes. It will make a nice keepsake for Rachel, but to tell you the truth, I’m not fond of staged portraits. I’d taken plenty of shots of her in action with everyone else before she posed for the camera.”

“Get them when they’re not looking.”

“Right.”

He took a sip of champagne. “I’d guess you heard Rachel when she wasn’t looking, too.”

“Her voice does carry, just like yours. She’s right about her dress. You won’t recognize your little girl tomorrow.”

“Don’t be too sure. I think I’d know her anywhere. But what about you—got any surprises for me?”

“What? Are you asking me to break my vow of silence?”

She’d sounded mocking, which didn’t match the way she stared past him as if his response didn’t matter. What *was* he asking? Not for promises or vows, broken or fulfilled. “No, you’re safe there.”

“Good, because I won’t tell you a thing. You’ll just have to wait and see.”

He smiled, already seeing what he wanted to see.

Then he stared a bit longer and saw something more.

He looked at her calm silver-gray eyes and envisioned them sparkling like the shimmery fabric of her dress. He noted the small, polite smile on her lips and imagined taking that mouth with his. He didn’t want to wait for whatever surprises she might have in store. He wanted to surprise her. To kiss her again. Right here. And right now.

Tearing his gaze away, he peered down into his glass in surprise.

Jed must have spent a bundle on some mighty potent champagne.

Jane left the noise-filled, crowded kitchen and stepped out onto the Hitching Post's back porch. It was late, after ten now, and a three-quarter moon hung overhead, drenching the ranch in silver light and dense shadows.

Somehow, she had managed to walk away calmly from Pete's table earlier that evening. Somehow, she had managed to keep her mind on her job. But when she least expected it, her thoughts would slip back to their conversation.

She was an expert at reading faces, and in the few short seconds that he'd sat staring at her, she had seen every thought that had come into his head.

Or maybe she chose to believe she knew what he wanted—because she wanted it, too.

Across the yard, one of the shadows shifted, separating from the dark hulk of the barn. When she caught sight of the outline of broad shoulders and a flash of light-colored hair, she descended the porch steps and crossed the open space.

Just as she had a couple of hours ago, she moved toward Pete calmly. Also like last time, though, her heart beat erratically. And now her pulse raced, too. Her camera still hung from its strap. She reached up to hold it, partly to keep it from bouncing against her as she crossed the yard, mostly to give her something to do with her hands.

He was still wearing the long-sleeved cowboy shirt and dress pants he'd worn to dinner earlier. She could still smell the musky aftershave that had made her want to stand closer to him as they walked down the chapel aisle.

In the days since they had kissed, she had thought about that pleasure more often than she'd intended, had craved it more than she'd ever thought she would. Now she felt a sudden hope her longing would be satisfied.

"You're out late," she said.

"Just checking on Starlight."

"Starlight in the moonlight?" she asked idiotically, stifling an urge to laugh.

"Starlight's a horse."

"Oh. I guess if I'd spent more time out here at the barn on my visits, I'd have known."

"Well..." He shrugged. "She's only been around for three years, so I'll give you a break on that."

She wished he would give her something else.

As if he'd taken a turn at reading thoughts, he moved closer and touched her sleeve. "Nice dress."

"That sounds a few steps down from 'pretty.'"

He laughed softly. "So, you *did* hear what Rachel and I said. Hoping to catch more compliments?"

"Maybe. Have I brought the right bait?"

"Maybe. Let's try it and see." He ran his hand up her arm, then to her shoulder. With one finger, he stroked the skin left exposed at the neckline of her dress, setting off ripples of pleasure inside her. "Smooth," he murmured.

He palmed the side of her neck, his long fingers tunneling into her hair, his thumb brushing her cheek. "Soft," he said.

"Trying to win me over with compliments, cowboy?"

"Maybe." He tilted her chin up and lowered his head, touched his lips all too briefly to hers. "Sweet," he said against her mouth.

He slipped his hand to the back of her head and held her still as he kissed her, fully, completely, leaving behind the faintest flavor of good champagne. Leaving her tingling all over.

"Satisfying," he said smugly.

If he only knew. "Is that another compliment for me," she murmured, "or a commentary on your technique?"

Smiling, he shrugged. "I'll let you be the judge of that."

He slid his arm around her, pulling her close.

The bulky weight of her camera, trapped between them, filled her with frustration. She wanted to get closer, to feel the heat from his body against hers.

He froze, stared at her for a long moment, then took a step back. He let her go, and the warmth of his arm gave way to a shot of cold reality.

He looked down at the camera. "Never leave home without it?"

She attempted a laugh. "It goes where I go. France. Argentina. South Africa."

"And little ol' Cowboy Creek."

Little *being the key word,* his expression seemed to say. He was right. She was grateful for the reminder. Cowboy Creek was not where she belonged, and this small-town rancher was not the guy for her.

Biting her tongue, she took a step back, too, and re-settled the camera against her.

"Raising your shield again?" he asked.

"Excuse me?"

"The camera." He gestured toward it. "I saw you with it tonight. I see you when we're together at the hotel. You use that camera as a way to protect yourself. You use all your high-tech toys to keep you from getting involved with folks."

"That's not true."

"Sure it is."

She ignored the sting of his words and fought to focus on their conversation. Hoping she could get through to him about his children, she pushed on. "I do connect with people, Pete, all over the world, outside my circle of family and close friends. Unlike you. Socializing only with everyone here on the ranch isn't doing you any good. More important, it's keeping your kids from making friends. And maybe from a relationship with their mother."

Even in the moonlight, she could see his jaw harden and his chest rise as he fought to take a calming breath. It was powerful proof that even a mention of his wife still affected him.

"Thanks for the thirty seconds of psychobabble," he snapped. "I hope you're not charging a lot for it, because you haven't said anything worth much."

She couldn't let the insult bother her. Not when, beneath the bitterness of his tone, she heard hurt and confusion. Yet she couldn't get past his defenses. Worst of all, no matter how she tried, she couldn't help him understand his daughter.

He shoved his hands into his pockets. "I talk plenty. To folks I can trust."

"Then," she said sadly, "I suggest you find one of them and have a heart-to-heart chat."

Chapter Eleven

After her conversation with Pete last night, Jane felt the need for some time alone. Or almost alone.

Early this morning, she had called Sharon to invite Rachel to breakfast at the Hitching Post. Tina's maid of honor joined them, too. The bridal party had scheduled hair and nail appointments for later that morning.

Rachel seemed overjoyed to hear that, until then, she would spend her time with Jane.

They had gone to the Hitching Post's small chapel to rehearse her walk down the aisle. Rachel had laughed at the idea of using paper clips to stand in for the rose petals.

"We have to save the flowers for the wedding today, right?" she had asked.

"Right," Jane had confirmed. "Smart girl."

One promise kept, now she was keeping another. She had brought her cameras—her high-tech toys, Pete called them—and some props to the honeymoon cabin.

Along with the renovations, Tina had budgeted for new linens and accessories for the little-used cabins. This one, refurbished by the contractors and now ready for a pair of newlyweds, held a four-poster bed with a gauzy white canopy, curtains and throw pillows, contrasting with the multicolored pastel bedspread and the matching fabric of the couch. The combination would photograph well for the website.

Rachel sat on the couch, watching everything. "Jane, can I have my nails polished like the big girls?"

She had noticed Sharon never wore nail polish and wondered if Rachel had ever had play polish to pretend with. It wasn't something her daddy might think of, but maybe Sharon had. "I don't see why we can't get your nails done."

"Yay!" Rachel ran to throw her arms around her.

The hug warmed her heart.

She smiled at Rachel, then got to work. With the little girl helping, she arranged the scene, down to and including candles on the nightstands, chocolates on the bed pillows and rose petals strewn across the pristine white sheets.

"I love chocolate," Rachel announced. "And Robbie loves chocolate, too."

"So do I," Jane admitted. "Would you like a piece?"

"Yes, please. And can I have a piece for Robbie?"

"Of course you can. That's very nice of you to share."

"I have to," Rachel said, so matter-of-factly Jane had to swallow a laugh. "Daddy told me. I practice that, too, like I practiced with the flowers."

"Good for you."

And good for Pete for teaching her so well.

She felt sure he was trying to fill the gap left by Rachel's absent mother, but that wasn't his only reason. All this week, she had watched him interact with his daughter and knew he would have been just as attentive even if Marina hadn't left. No matter his reasons for not wanting the photo shoot yesterday, he was a thoroughly wonderful daddy.

And an equally wonderful man.

She had just finished her first round of photos when the door behind her opened. Though she had no logical reason to know who had stepped into the cabin, her senses told her it was Pete.

With a glance, Pete took in the scene inside the cabin. Candy, flowers, Rachel…and Jane. One sight of her by the bed, and his imagination took flight.

"Hi, Daddy!" Rachel ran to give him a hug. "Do you see what Jane and me did? Isn't the bed pretty? Jane gave me some chocolate, and I said 'please.'"

"That's my girl."

"And," Jane said, "she asked to share a piece with Robbie."

He smiled and ruffled his daughter's hair.

"I practiced with the flowers," she said. "Jane told me I did a good job."

"Great. You'll be all ready for this afternoon."

Over Rachel's head, Jane's gaze met his coolly—which was probably the reaction he deserved. It looked like, in his hair-trigger jump to protective mode, he had misjudged her.

He smiled, trying to convey an apology without words.

"What brings you here?" she asked.

You. The response came automatically, but he had sense enough not to say it aloud. The last thing he'd said to her yesterday ensured that kiss had been their last. He had no hope for anything else.

Just as well.

"Tina asked me to give you a message," he said. And he'd jumped at the chance. "She wants to head into town early to stop in at SugarPie's."

"All right. We'll finish up here."

She fidgeted with her camera as if she couldn't wait to get back to her task. He didn't doubt she was counting the days until her photos for the website were all done and she could leave Cowboy Creek behind her.

AT A TABLE for four in SugarPie's, Jane sat across from Tina and Andi. Close by, Rachel and Robbie and Trey, Andi's son, sat at a smaller table, coloring with the crayons Sugar provided for her younger customers.

Tina's future sister-in-law, Layne, had come to wait on their table. Cole had stayed the night with the single mom and her young son at her apartment.

Tradition, Jed had insisted. *Can't have the groom seeing the bride before the wedding.*

"Cole made it through the night," Layne assured them all with a laugh. "I'm taking the afternoon off, and I'll make sure he's at the Hitching Post on time." She brushed her hand across her protruding stomach. "Scott's already talking about getting to see his mama and Uncle Cole all dressed up. To tell you the truth, I'm happy for a reason to break out my dancing shoes, too."

Her smile said she meant it, but the dark circles under her eyes indicated her pregnancy might be interfering with a good night's sleep. When Jane had last visited Cowboy Creek, Layne had just taken on extra hours at the shop, and according to Tina, she was still working overtime as often as she could. Jane hoped the evening out would do Layne some good.

"It's nice you're getting a break, with it so quiet in here," Jane said, "but isn't that unusual on a Saturday?"

"You've just come at the right time," Layne said. "Things will pick up soon. In fact, I'd better go put your orders in before the crowd gets here." She went back toward the kitchen.

"It won't stay quiet at this table for long," Andi said. "I can see Missy getting ready to fuss. I'm going to walk her outside and up Canyon Road a bit. I can meet Ally on her way here from the store." She set the baby into her portable stroller.

"Let Ally know we've already got her sandwich on order."

"And don't get lost," Jane said, forcing a laugh. "We can't have the bride showing up late at the salon." She watched Andi leave the shop, then turned back to find Tina eyeing her over the rim of her teacup.

"Something wrong?" Tina asked.

"You've changed, coz," Jane said bluntly. "Once, you wouldn't have asked that question."

"Once, I didn't know you as well. And I have to say, now that you're on your second trip here in mere months, I'm getting used to having you around."

"Don't do that." She smiled. "You know I'm headed back to New York in another week."

"And we're leaving for Disneyland tomorrow."

Until the renovations were done, Tina and Cole had opted to postpone their official honeymoon, but now that they were together as a family, they wanted to spend a few days alone with Robbie.

Tina had gotten her happy-ever-after. Andi still grieved for her husband but had two kids she loved. Even Pete, despite his situation with his ex-wife, had formed a tight-knit family with Rachel and Eric. And she...

Well, she had the career she had always wanted. Somebody had to be willing to step outside the box.

Tina cleared her throat, sending Jane's wandering thoughts back to her. "Anything you want to talk about with me while you still have the chance? I won't say a word to anyone—you know that."

She did know. Slowly, she admitted, "I'm concerned about Rachel."

"Did you get in touch with Marina?"

"Not yet. I'm planning to send her a message through her website."

"And what about Pete?"

"What about him?"

"Well..." Tina gave a soft laugh. "When I looked through the kitchen window last night, I saw you outside with him."

To her annoyance, she felt her cheeks warm. "Did you?"

"Yes. And I wish you luck." Tina smiled. "Call me Pollyanna, but I'm so happy right now, I guess I want everyone else to feel the same."

"You should be happy. I'm happy for you. But whatever I have on my mind, it has nothing to do with Pete."

Tina had just taken another sip of tea, and her eyebrows rose above the cup's rim.

"Oh, all right." She sighed. Normally, she didn't confide her personal problems, and she didn't often have the occasion to share girl talk with anyone. But Tina, her quiet cousin, was trustworthy, not one to spread gossip, and she knew Pete. And she *was* leaving tomorrow.

Leaning closer to the table and keeping her voice low, she said, "Pete's driving me crazy." She gave the bare-bones version of what she had said to him the night before. "He can't accept that what he's doing might be hurting his kids."

"Maybe there's more to it than you can see."

"Then why wouldn't he tell me?"

"Because he's a private person, remember? I can certainly understand that." Tina set her teacup on the table. "But maybe there's more to it on your side, too?"

"Like what?"

"I don't know, but from what I saw last night—and

don't worry, I only got a glimpse, I promise you—he was driving you crazy in a good way."

Jane flushed again, more from the memory than the thought of Tina observing them.

"Maybe you'd better analyze how you feel about that."

"Says Tina, the hotel bookkeeper." She smiled to soften the words. "You're the expert with the analyses and spreadsheets."

"You're the pro at getting to the heart of people. Maybe you ought to think of this in those terms."

The shop door opened. Ally and Andi entered with the baby.

"Don't forget what I said," Tina urged quietly. "Think about it."

"I will. And don't forget what else you said. You're leaving on your trip tomorrow. So, no long-distance calls from Cinderella's castle to see if I've done my homework."

They both laughed and sat back as Layne approached the table with their lunch order.

Andi and Ally took their seats.

As the three other women talked, Jane tried to follow the conversation, but her mind was already busy with Tina's suggestion, analyzing how and why and what she felt when it came to Pete.

Get to the heart, her cousin had said.

That was always her goal. *When you're focusing intently on the big picture,* her first-year professor cautioned, *don't forget all the important, telling details.*

Getting to the heart of a subject, for her, always included visuals. In her mind, she saw plenty of images of Pete. She saw him striding from the barn with the bright sunshine on his light brown hair. Standing in the moonlight leaning toward her for a kiss. Watching his daughter with love and pride in his eyes. She saw him pensive and frustrated, thoughtful and happy, irritated and elated—all through the lens of her camera, though she hadn't always taken the shots.

In all those scenes, she saw a man who intrigued her and made her want to learn more. But she couldn't seem to reach the heart of him.

While he, on the other hand, had already gotten to *her* heart.

PETE STOOD IN the small chapel between his fellow usher and Cole's best man as the rest of the wedding party took their walk down the aisle.

His first sight of Jane left him breathless.

She had done something to make her dark hair look even softer and shinier. Instead of her usual silver jewelry, she wore a strand of pearls. And…

He struggled to take a breath.

He had known she'd look good in something other than those loose black shirts she always wore. But *this*… The deep blue gown left her shoulders and arms bare, plunged down the front and skimmed over her hips. As beautiful as she looked in the gown, he felt the urge to strip it off her. At that thought, his entire body tightened, and he only hoped he wouldn't embarrass himself in front of everyone attending the wedding.

As she reached the first in the small row of pews, she smiled at the groom. Pete waited for her to send that smile his way. She didn't. She turned and took her place beside Andi, followed by Ally.

After another deep breath, he looked down the aisle again. Robbie walked carefully, holding a pillow with two attached rings.

At the chapel entrance, Rachel stood waiting for some

cue. A moment later, she started down the aisle in the gown she had been so excited about wearing. He hadn't seen her since his trip to the cabin. Her cheeks were rosy with excitement, and her eyes sparkled. One by one, she dropped her rose petals as serenely as if she had done it a million times. His vision blurred. He had to blink to clear his eyes.

As she reached the front pew, she gave him a smile as bright as the one Jane had denied him.

This close, he saw her rosy cheeks had gotten some help from makeup. He felt certain Jane had something to do with that. Once he got her alone, he'd make a point of sharing his thoughts about it.

He smiled at Rachel, then watched her take her place. As the "Wedding March" began, he turned his attention to the chapel entrance.

He had never seen Jed in a tuxedo. He'd never seen Tina look so happy.

His thoughts flew to Rachel again. Disregarding the makeup she wore, he focused on recalling her composure as she'd made her trip down the aisle.

No matter how he felt about Jane at that very moment, he couldn't help but thank her silently for the morning rehearsal with his daughter.

Chapter Twelve

In the banquet hall of the Hitching Post, Jed looked around him, taking stock of the room. He felt justifiably proud of the progress his granddaughters had made. Everything in the place sparkled, from the crystals in the chandeliers to the champagne glasses on the tables.

"It's so beautiful," Paz said.

He nodded his agreement.

The guests, now trickling into the room after their walk from the chapel, all seemed ready to have a good time.

So was Jed. He felt justifiably proud of his own progress, too, slow as it might be.

The bride and groom approached on their way to the head table. Tina stopped beside him and kissed his cheek. "Don't forget to save me a dance, my handsome *abuelo*."

He patted her arm. "Don't you worry about that, girl. I've got a space on my dance card just for you."

Cole's best man clapped him on the shoulder, and the two turned aside to talk.

Jed shot another look around him, and this time, he frowned. "Jane's on one side of the room. Pete's on the other," he grumbled.

"Give them time," Tina said. "They just came into the hall."

"Time is the one thing I don't have much of. What do you think, Paz? Should I light a fire under Pete?"

She smiled. "I don't know if that will be necessary. You were still at the back of the chapel when Jane walked down the aisle. For certain, I would say at that moment Pete already had a fire inside him."

"And Jane?"

"She deliberately didn't look at him. I think that's a good sign."

"You do?"

She nodded.

"So do I," Tina said. "It's called playing hard to get."

"It's what I call making it hard to get them together," he grumbled. "I may just take a walk and see if I can't do something about that."

"DADDY, DON'T I look pretty?"

Pete stood with Rachel and Sharon, who held Eric in her arms.

Rachel twirled, making the skirt of her blue dress billow around her. Her eyes were sparkling, her cheeks pink, her blond hair held back with a flowered band.

Pete smiled. "You look gorgeous."

"Thank you. Did you see my nails?" She waggled her fingers, showing off the pale pink polish.

"Very pretty," Sharon said. "And, Pete, didn't she do a fantastic job walking down the aisle in the chapel?"

"She sure did." He winked at the older woman. "Except she kept dropping her flowers."

"Daddy! You know I was *supposed* to drop them!"

Laughing, he kissed Rachel's forehead. "Well, in that case, you did a great job there, too."

"Uh-huh. I have to go find my seat now. I'm at the big table in the front with the other girls." She turned to

Sharon and added, "Daddy's sitting at the big table with me. I'm sorry you and Eric can't sit there."

Sharon smiled. "That's fine, Rachel. Eric and I have seats at the round table right next to you. We'll have no problem seeing you and your daddy."

"And the bride, too? Because Tina's the star."

"Yes, we'll see the bride, too."

"Good. Okay, see you later. I have to find Robbie and tell him where to sit."

He and Sharon laughed as they watched her weave her way among the guests.

"I guess I've got to have another talk with her about that bossiness," he said. But at least she had remembered this was Tina's big day.

Sharon smiled. "Look how concerned she was about where I'd sit with Eric. She's coming along, and you're doing an excellent job with her."

I can tell what a good father you are, Jane had said. *I can see you're doing a wonderful job.*

Her comment had given him the same pleasure Sharon's did now. "Thanks."

When she went to find her seat, Pete attempted a casual scan of the crowd, hoping it didn't look obvious he was searching for someone.

"Hey, Pete!"

At the sound of Jed's voice behind him, pitched to rise above the music, he turned to find his boss beaming at him. With his white hair and dark tuxedo and the extra trappings in the same shade of blue as Jane's dress, he looked dapper and fit and, as Jed himself would say, "pleased as punch."

He ought to be happy, as he'd been the man to walk Tina down the aisle. The only one of the three cousins with no parents, she had had the choice of two uncles to do the honors. Maybe to avoid having to choose between them, she had asked Jed to walk with her. He doubted that was the only reason. Tina and Jed had always shared a special bond.

If Cole's story about Jed playing matchmaker had been true, then the old man had more than one reason to look so pleased tonight. But that was a topic Pete wasn't about to touch on.

"What are you doing over here by your lonesome?" Jed asked.

"Chatting with Rachel and Sharon. They just went to find their seats."

Jed looked toward the front of the room and nodded. "I see Jane's up at the head table. You'd better keep an eye on her."

He would do that, all right. Ever since the bridal party had entered the banquet hall, he hadn't caught her alone. He wanted a private conversation with her about Rachel and that makeup.

Now he followed Jed's gaze and found her by the table.

Every time he looked her way, his entire body jumped to attention.

"The two of you need to be ready to shake a leg," Jed continued. "The bride and groom will be the floor show in just a few minutes, and then you'll need to join them. I'll take Tina for a whirl a little while later."

"Sounds good."

Jed gave him a wave and moved off.

Pete looked back at the head table, only to find that Jane had disappeared.

He scanned the crowd again, looking for one particular woman in a bright blue gown. When he spotted her near the drinks table with Andi and Cole's sister, Layne, he promptly headed in that direction.

JANE TOOK ANOTHER sip of her punch and smiled at Andi and Layne. The two women had come up to get drinks of their own and stayed to chat.

"Your gowns are beautiful," Layne said. "And you two and Ally all look wonderful."

"Thanks," Jane said. "You look great yourself." Layne wore a long-sleeved dress in turquoise that went well with her light brown hair and made her eyes bluer. Jane knew just the shot she'd want to take of the expectant mom. "I can picture you in a portrait…in profile…with soft lighting…"

Pete had accused her of hiding behind her camera. Though his statement wasn't true, she winced at the memory.

"You don't know how much I thank you for saying that." Layne laughed and rested her hand on her rounded stomach. "This dress isn't quite as roomy as the uniform at SugarPie's, but it was the only thing I had to wear."

"I know that feeling," Andi said, rolling her eyes.

Jane smiled at her cousin's fib. Andi, whose husband had come from a well-to-do family, would have had maternity clothes that fit her every inch of the way. But she and Andi both knew about Layne's circumstances.

"In fact," Andi added, "I've got so many maternity clothes from when I was carrying Missy. You know how fast babies grow when they start nearing full-term. I had to keep buying bigger sizes. Layne, I'd love to send you some of them."

"Thanks, but I couldn't accept."

"Of course you could. I don't plan to use them again. You'd be doing me a favor by helping me clear out my closet."

Another fib. In her large home, Andi also had a surplus of storage space.

Andi smiled. "And don't forget, as of today, we're all officially family. Cousins-in-law."

"Through marriage," Layne clarified, but her blue eyes were bright. She squeezed Andi's arm. "Thanks," she said softly. "Cole and Tina offered to help me out, and I'll let them if I have to, but I didn't want to rely on them for things I can do without."

"A woman always needs some nice clothes and makeup," Jane said.

The two women started a conversation about childbirth that Jane could take no part in. Smiling, she let her thoughts drift. The mention of makeup had made her think of Pete's daughter. Rachel had been so happy about her pale pink polished nails, Jane had added a light dusting of blush to her cheeks.

Thinking of Rachel automatically drew her thoughts to Pete.

After a quick glance around the banquet hall, she found him standing on the opposite side of the dance floor. He looked so tall and broad-shouldered and handsome in his fitted tux, her hand itched to close around her camera. But Tina and Cole had forbidden that for this evening. Her cousins knew her better than she knew herself.

Before she could glance away, Pete looked in her direction. Her gaze met his, and even at that distance, she felt the connection like a touch.

A moment later, she *did* feel a touch. Andi had lightly prodded her in the ribs. Turning, she saw with surprise that Andi now stood alone. "What happened to Layne?"

"She needed to sit down for a bit. And that was *a while* ago." Andi's brows rose. "Something catch your attention?"

"Just scanning the crowd. You know me—I'm always on the lookout for new faces."

"One particular face tonight, you mean. I saw who you were looking at. Robbie and Rachel would tell you it's not nice to fib."

"Listen to you. Didn't I hear you telling Layne you've got no room for your maternity clothes?"

"That wasn't a fib." For a moment, shadows filled Andi's eyes. "I'm selling the house. The kids and I have moved into an apartment."

"Oh. Andi, I didn't know."

"And it's not important right now. What is of interest is the way you were staring at Pete."

"I was *not* staring." Still, she blushed.

"Uh-huh. Just as Pete would probably deny watching you in the chapel. He didn't even look at me when I came down the aisle. He only had eyes for you. I'm telling you the truth, Jane. That man could be yours. If you're willing to go get him."

"Oh, please." As hard as she tried to laugh off Andi's statement, she couldn't. She also couldn't help glancing across the room again. Jed and Pete had moved on. As she looked through the crowd, she saw him making his way in their direction.

His steady gaze said he was coming to get *her*.

AS PETE NEARED JANE, she gave him a smile that looked great from a distance. At close range, it seemed fixed in place.

From beneath the strands of her hair, diamond earrings winked at him in the light. She held up a crystal glass that winked at him, too. Both only taunted him when all he wanted was to see a sparkle in her eyes.

Andi had drifted away, leaving Jane standing alone. "Would you like some punch?" she asked.

As he accepted the glass he said, "I'd also like a word."

"That sounds serious."

He took her elbow, the way he had in the chapel. This time, instead of walking her down the center of the room, he stepped with her to one side, nearer to the band and the loud music that would give their conversation the cover of privacy. It also gave him a reason to stand close to her.

The scent of her perfume reached him. A new scent. Tonight she had dropped the vanilla and stayed with pure spice, subtle but with enough of a kick to wake up his senses.

In many good ways, she managed to get his attention. But he had no time now for pleasure. Or politeness.

"Rachel and the makeup," he said abruptly. "Your idea, I suppose?"

"I had a feeling you'd ask. Yes. She had her nails done with the rest of us this morning, and I couldn't resist letting her try a little blush."

"I wish you'd tried harder not to follow through. You don't know much about being a parent, do you?"

"Of course I don't. But you could stop being such a cowpoke for once, can't you? For heaven's sake, she's the flower girl. Today's a very special day for Rachel. Maybe a once-in-a-lifetime event. And when she's flushed with excitement, the way she's been all night, you can't even notice the blush."

"She's a five-year-old."

"Many little girls dress up and wear a tiny bit of makeup when they're in a wedding party. I was thinking of how much she would enjoy it. And of how pretty she'd look in the photos and video."

"Life is not about getting all dolled up for pictures. At least, my life isn't. Can't you see anything that doesn't show up through your camera lens?"

"How can you miss so many things right in front of

your eyes?" She gave him a brilliant smile probably intended only for the blasted photographer. "Maybe if you'd take the blinders off, you'd see what I mean."

"And that's all that matters, isn't it?"

Before he could stop her, she turned and slipped away.

Damn.

The woman wasn't going to listen to reason. Wasn't going to give him the benefit of the doubt. Probably wasn't going to drop the subject permanently until he had bared his soul.

He loathed the idea of making more explanations. And he sure wasn't going to continue taking her interference in the way he was raising his kids.

But he couldn't risk her making trouble for him with Jed—and that had nothing to do with his debt or his job or his home on Garland Ranch. No way would he let her ruin his standing with his boss because she'd gotten a wild idea in her head and wouldn't let go.

He'd have to reveal more of his private life to her. He'd have to tell her things he didn't want to share.

HOW SHE WAS going to manage to get through this evening, she didn't know.

After watching the bride and groom complete their first solo dance as husband and wife, Jane and the rest of the bridal party joined them on the dance floor. When Pete put his arm around her, she stiffened and nearly tripped over her own feet.

They danced together without speaking, and the silence felt almost worse than having to talk. She could sense the conversation they had had such a short while ago hanging in the air like the moon that had hovered above them last night.

She forced her thoughts away and concentrated on

the music. Soon, she found the drumbeats keeping time with the thumps of her heart. The rippling piano keys matched her racing pulse. The ragged notes of the saxophone echoed her uneven breathing.

A glance upward made her realize her excitement hadn't come from the music at all. Pete stood looking down at her, and everything—heart, pulse, breath—immediately revved up.

"You're hanging on to that frozen smile tonight no matter what, aren't you?" he asked.

She was grateful for this proof she hadn't given away her reactions. "You bet I am, cowboy. Later tonight, I might need to borrow an ice pick from Paz's kitchen to chip this smile off my face. I'm not going to ruin Tina and Cole's big night. No matter what."

No matter how tempted she felt to walk away from this man. No matter how much he tempted her to want other things.

How could he both fascinate and irritate her at the same time?

He shifted his hand against her back, bared by the halter top of her dress, and his warmth spread everywhere he touched. He flexed his fingers, spreading them in a quick, gentle massage, the action most likely unintentional but enough to send his heat all through her.

How could she feel both that warmth and a chill at the same time?

"Let's take a walk," he said. "I've got something to say to you."

And how could she want to say no and yes, all at the same time?

She'd never been this indecisive in her life. But this she knew for sure: she wanted to hear whatever he intended to say.

He looked as indecisive as she felt. She shouldn't read anything into that.

As the song ended, he escorted her from the dance floor. She matched her stride to his—a stride she suspected he had adjusted on her behalf, as her slim gown and high heels considerably limited her steps.

Her mother, seated with Jed, gave them a wave.

Halfway across the room, they met her father. From her viewpoint as both his daughter and a photographer, he was a handsome man. His military haircut couldn't hide the salt and pepper of his hair—more salt since she had last seen her parents nearly a year ago. That, along with his tuxedo, increased his resemblance to Jed.

He nodded to Pete. "I'll take Jane off your hands for a while. It's about time I have a dance with my daughter."

"Fine by me," Pete said.

He faked a smile for her father's sake, she knew. She wanted it to be real and for her. And as much as she would enjoy the dance with her father, she wished it could wait until she found out what Pete had on his mind.

Out on the dance floor, her father said, "It's nice being home again, even if for a short time. You should give some thought to settling down in the area."

She laughed. "Sounds like you've been talking to Grandpa."

"He's not making a secret of the fact he wants more of the family around him. And you know I won't be retiring anytime soon."

"Neither will I, and I've got more years than you to go."

"You travel so much, you could make the ranch your home base."

She shook her head. "Cowboy Creek could never offer me the opportunities I have in New York. I've got the contacts and a reputation there. When I'm not traveling and want to pick up work in the city, I can choose my own jobs."

"You've done well for yourself, Jane." He squeezed her hand. "Your mother and I are very proud of you."

Instantly, she thought of Pete's pride for Rachel.

She smiled. Though she knew her father loved her, he had never been generous with praise, unlike her mother. "Thanks. I'm pretty proud of you both, too."

When the dance ended, they walked to the refreshment table for a drink. Pete sat at a table not far away, with Eric on his lap and Rachel and Sharon on either side. Whatever he wanted to tell her, it would have to wait a while longer. Maybe indefinitely, if he had changed his mind.

Her father glanced around the banquet hall. "Looks very good in here."

"Thanks to Tina. She took care of lining up all the contractors. And she's still keeping track of everything."

"It will be some time before the renovations are done completely."

She nodded. The band had taken a break, and over the hum of conversations she heard Rachel's laugh. At the table, Pete smiled and leaned down to kiss her forehead.

Her father had noticed, too. "Good man, that Pete. Your granddad's always thought a lot of him."

"Yes," she murmured. She had thought a lot of *and* about him lately.

You're the pro at getting to the heart of people, she reminded herself. Or so Tina had said.

Getting to the heart of a subject always meant getting to know the person through interviews and casual conversation until she found the angle she wanted to pursue.

Getting to know Pete reinforced another conclusion she'd come to at their meeting in the barn last week. Both when he was alone with her and when he interacted with his kids, she saw a lot of her father in him. She saw love and caring and concern in both men, but she also noted the need for control surfaced differently in each of them.

Her dad might be a strict commanding officer—not surprising, she had finally come to realize, considering his rank and responsibilities. While that sometimes filtered into his own life, for the most part, he relied on that discipline to lead his troops.

Pete had turned his control onto himself. He had set much narrower boundaries for his life, managing to keep to them by refusing to discuss his ex-wife and not acknowledging his daughter's needs.

In trying to maintain those boundaries, had he lost sight of what really mattered?

Chapter Thirteen

The wedding reception had ended, the bride and groom had left to pack for their quick trip with Robbie, the two visiting groomsmen had gone to their rooms upstairs, and Sharon had taken his kids over to the house.

And still Pete sat in the Hitching Post's banquet hall with Jed and his family.

He, along with the rest of the men in the room, had undone his tie and the top button of his tuxedo shirt. Jed had given up on the cummerbund altogether and draped it over the back of his chair.

Andi and Jane had joined Andi's father and Jane's parents at their table. He and Jed and Paz were at the one adjacent to it.

"What do you say, Paz?" Jed asked. "Did we do right by the bride and groom, or did we not?"

"We did." She gave him a smile so broad, her full cheeks nudged her eyes into a squint.

"You outdid yourself with the dinner," Pete told her.

She patted his arm. "Thank you, but it was nothing. Tina and Cole wanted a buffet menu, and that was easy. The same as I make for the dining room, except increasing the recipes for the number of guests."

"And Sugar did the cake and all the trimmings. Hey,

Jane," Jed called over to her, "what did you think about the desserts? Not bad, huh?"

She sat only a few feet from Pete, her chair angled slightly away from him. "You need to put Sugar on the banquet hall's vendor list," she said. "Her desserts were delicious."

She was delicious, and he needed to get his arms around her again. He hadn't managed to get her alone since their turn on the dance floor.

Jed looked around the banquet hall and gave an approving nod. "We'll be ready to start taking reservations for this room soon," he announced to the group. "And I don't know about you boys—" he turned to look at his sons "—but I think it's high time we have another wedding in the family. Jane, you're the oldest. What do you think?"

"We haven't quite wrapped up this wedding yet," she said. "And if you mean you're looking for me to be next in the lineup, I'm afraid you're out of luck. Once I leave here next week, it's back to work, and my schedule's full for at least the next three years."

"Yeah, we need to talk about that schedule. C'mon on over here for a minute, will you?"

"Sure."

Andi and the others at the table went back to their conversation. Jane came to sit on the far side of the table from Pete. While he would have liked her by his side, he didn't mind the current seating arrangements, either. He could look directly across the table at her and watch every move she made.

"This schedule of yours," Jed said, frowning. "You'll be back again here soon, won't you? We'll want you to start work on the website."

"There's no need for me to be here for that, Grandpa.

I'll have all the photos taken by the time I go, and from then on, I can do everything on the computer."

So, she didn't plan to stick around, not even to help Jed and her cousins with the rest of the hotel renovations. Here today, gone as soon as possible. An all-too-familiar story.

Like his ex, she was all about what she wanted, about what was best for her. Maybe she wasn't abandoning her family the way Marina had, but not pitching in to help was a parallel, one much too close for him to ignore. For her, the career came first.

"The website is the kind of job I can do when I'm flying between assignments," she told Jed. "Believe me, I have plenty of downtime waiting at airports. And most of my assignments involve long international flights."

Yeah. *France. Argentina. South Africa.*

In conversation, she mentioned travel to different countries the way his father dropped the names of well-known organizations. The way Marina used to talk about the ritzy locations of her fashion shows.

Jane would never give up her globe-trotting to settle down.

"What about the videos?" Jed asked.

She nodded. "Summertime's perfect for scenic backgrounds here, so I'll get those done this week, too. I thought I'd start shooting on Monday, since Mom and Dad will be gone."

Gone? There went his hope of having her parents around for a while to keep her occupied—and him off the hook about playing her assistant. To keep him from trailing after her like some lovesick teenager.

"Good." Jed smiled. "Pete can drive you around to some likely places."

And the trip could drive him crazy.

He tugged at the tie hanging open at his neck. Bad idea, since his movement attracted Jed's eye. But hell, if what Cole had said about the boss's matchmaking was true, Jed would hunt him down to help Jane anyway. And then would draw and quarter him if he didn't comply.

JANE SLIPPED AWAY from the banquet hall, leaving her family involved in their post-wedding conversation.

Pete had left just moments ago and, though she never would admit it to him, she couldn't wait another minute to find out what he had wanted to tell her at the reception.

She ran the risk of his sharing something she didn't want to hear. But despite this, and the night air still warm from the New Mexico summer heat, she couldn't fight off a small shiver of anticipation.

Outside, she saw him walking across the yard to his own house. She called his name softly. He turned back, hesitated, then met her near the steps. "We never did finish our talk," she reminded him.

"No, we didn't." He reached up to run his hand through his hair, golden in the glow of the porch light. His tuxedo jacket flapped open, revealing the starched and pleated white shirt straining against his chest and the blue cummerbund securely wrapped around his waist.

Things would soon change between them, she knew, when he found out what she had done. After her conversation with Tina, she had contacted Marina and was waiting for a return email.

But for now, she was here, he was hers, and that was all she could think about.

That man could be yours. If you're willing to go get him.

She *was* willing.

She trailed her fingertips down the front of his shirt.

He reached up, trapping her hand against his chest. She could feel his heat. She could feel his heartbeat. She could feel something inside her that had gone all soft and warm.

"You really do clean up nice," she whispered, her voice shaking.

"For a cowboy, you mean?"

"No. For any man."

"You pretty up well yourself. For any man who might look, including this one. But I didn't expect..." He paused.

"Didn't expect what?"

"This wasn't..."

"Wasn't what?"

"Aw, hell, Jane. I don't know." He gave a low laugh and shook his head. "But for sure I don't want a game of Twenty Questions. Not this minute."

"What *do* you want?"

"You."

He took his hands on a slow ride up the length of her arms. She shivered again. He curled his fingers around her shoulders and gave another gentle tug. She accepted the unspoken invitation, letting him hold her close. Closer than he had on the dance floor. Close enough to feel his heat. He moved his hands to her shoulders once again, holding her steady as he bent his head for a long, sweet, satisfying kiss.

When they broke away, she felt ashamed of needing a deep breath—until the moonlight showed her the answering rise and fall of his pleated white shirt.

"I didn't mean to do that," he said hoarsely.

"Of course not," she murmured. "Just like when I told my father I didn't mean to drop the cookie jar on the kitchen floor. It was an accident."

"And he believed you."

"Absolutely. He knew I never lied to him. But I did

have quite a time explaining how the kitchen chair had overturned and why the door of the cabinet where my mother hid the cookie jar was hanging wide open." She laughed softly.

He ran his hand along her arm again. "And I thought I had a time of it with Rachel and her antics."

"Wait till Eric gets older. I hear little boys are worse."

"So Cole and Tina tell me."

"Well. Now that we've done—" she waved her hand between them "—*this*, have you figured out what you wanted?"

"I told you that already. I want you. But the hotel's full of your family, and Sharon's home now with the kids." He laughed and shook his head. "And I can hardly take you to the barn in *this* dress." He ran both hands down her sides and over her hips, pulling her against him, leaving her with no doubt about how much he wanted her.

This time, his kiss was longer, deeper, hotter, but didn't leave her satisfied at all.

"The cabin's still open," she whispered.

He smiled. "And I can't let you walk there through the grass in those shoes."

In one swift motion, he swept her up in his arms.

She shivered yet again, this time at the irony of the night. Her one and only time with him would be in a honeymoon haven.

INSIDE THE CABIN, Jane closed the door behind them. Before she could turn around, Pete had slipped his arms around her and placed a kiss on the back of her neck. That first touch became a series that trailed along her spine to the top of her gown.

She turned in his arms to find him staring down at her, his hazel-green eyes looking dazed. Without a word, he lifted her chin to take her mouth as if their last kiss had never ended. As if he didn't plan to finish it anytime soon.

Finally, he pulled back to stare into her eyes again. She gulped a ragged breath and said, "That wasn't bad at all."

He laughed roughly. "I could go for something better."

"If you must."

How he could kiss her any more thoroughly, she didn't know. But she was ready and willing to give him a chance. When he lowered his head, she parted her lips. Instead of meeting them with his own, he pressed a kiss against the pulse point at the side of her neck.

She gave a low, surprised gasp.

He gave a low, satisfied chuckle. Again, he pulled back to meet her gaze. "So, what's going on here?" he asked.

"We're making out."

He laughed. "I don't mean *here*—" he stroked her lips with his thumb "—I mean *here*." He gestured toward the bed.

"You ought to know the signs by now." She swallowed another surprised gasp at her own words.

She should have recognized the signs. Her signs. Her struggle to stay away from Pete. Her inability to tell him she no longer needed his help. Her caring. Her concern. Her worry. The conflicting emotions she hadn't yet acknowledged. The soft warmth that filled her heart.

And, above all, the truth she didn't want to face.

Her hand trembling, she copied his gesture toward the bed. "I was staging a seduction scene."

"I've got a better idea."

"Such as?"

"Forget the staging. Let's go for some live action."

No shivers now. A sizable tremor ran through her. Praying he hadn't noticed, she quickly forced a laugh. "That's a bit abrupt, isn't it?"

"All right, then. Let's start with the chocolates I see on those pillows."

He unwrapped one and fed it to her, the way he had the strawberry. She took a bite. He took the rest. They ate another. And another.

"You *do* like sweets, don't you?" he said.

"I know something sweeter," she whispered.

He groaned, then swept her into his arms again and carried her to the bed.

His lips now tasted like chocolate. Could there be anything better? When he pressed his mouth against the hollow of her throat, she knew there could.

As he'd done by the door, he left a trail of kisses down her body. Only this time, it led all the way to the bottom of the plunging neckline.

And this time, when he reached her gown, he kept going.

Chapter Fourteen

"It was a beautiful wedding, Jed." Still dressed in her finery, a teary-eyed Paz stood near the kitchen sink.

"It was indeed. And a productive one, as far as we're concerned. Tina and Cole married, and Jane and Pete tearing up the dance floor. Can't ask for more than that. Yet." His smile faded. "But just where the heck has that girl gotten to now?"

He and Paz had come to get a refill for the ice bucket and some additional drinks. Most of his family still sat around the tables in the banquet hall. All but the bride and groom and their son. And Jane.

"When I walked into the kitchen earlier," Paz said, "I saw her on the porch."

"Doing what?"

"Just standing and looking out to the yard."

"How much earlier was that?"

"Just after she left from the hall." She smiled. "Which was just after Pete had gone, too."

He laughed. "Are you thinking what I'm thinking about why they both disappeared?"

"I hope so."

"Good." He rattled the ice bucket. "Now the wedding's over, we don't have much time. Jane will be looking to go back to her job soon, and we've got to find a way to stop her."

"Maybe Pete will do that tonight while they're out walking in the moonlight."

"I reckon they might be up to more than that. But regardless, we've got to pick up the pace."

"How?"

"I don't know right now. But don't you worry—I'll think of something."

WITH COLE GONE away for a few days with his bride and their son, Pete had planned to work one man short. Since Jed hadn't booked any reservations for the upcoming week, either, except for family and a few of the wedding guests, that wouldn't pose a problem.

But to his surprise, bright and early on Sunday morning, Cole's best man, Tyler, showed up in the barn. And he wanted to work.

"Are you pulling my leg?" Pete asked, though he knew Tyler had the background and experience to do anything on the ranch. He set down the reins he'd been checking over and leaned his back against the workbench. "Cole said you were planning to hang around for a couple of days, taking a vacation. You're welcome to saddle up any of the mounts here. With it being a quiet week, the exercise will do them good."

"Yeah, well, I was thinking about a deal."

"Such as?"

"I want to go into town later today, but I haven't got wheels. Thought I'd put in a few hours working with you, and then maybe you and your kids might want to take a ride. I'll spring for dessert."

Pete laughed. "Dessert, huh? I'm thinking you don't mean the kind we had last night, from SugarPie's."

"No."

"And I'm thinking you're looking more for a good excuse to stop in at the Big Dipper."

The other man grinned. "You got it."

Pete nodded. He'd seen the man hitting on Shay the night of the bachelor party, then dancing with her at the reception. In fact, he wouldn't have been surprised if that had led to Tyler's decision to stick around the ranch.

"Why not?" he told Tyler. "And don't worry about working off the ride. My kids are due for a trip for some ice cream."

Overdue, if he told the truth.

He gave the man a tour of the stalls and his pick of a horse.

When Tyler had saddled up and left, Pete turned back to his work. He liked hanging around the barn on early Sunday mornings after the chores were done. He spent time on things he couldn't normally fit into his schedule. Paperwork, which he despised. Cleaning tack, which relaxed him. Inventory, which had to be done whether he liked it or not. But mostly, whatever the chore, he liked the quiet, broken only by the sound of a neighing horse or a barking dog. Or the arrival of the occasional human visitor, such as Tyler.

Or the woman standing in the doorway now.

"Thought you'd still be sleeping in," he said to Jane. Her blush, a reminder of her flushed face and rapid breaths the night before, made him hard. Recalling what they had done made him want her even more.

Also thanks to what they had done, he had never brought up the subject he'd intended to discuss with her at the reception. But now, maybe confessing more than he wanted to share wouldn't be necessary.

"I had breakfast with my mother and father," she said.

"They have an early flight out, so they're going to the airport with Tina and Cole."

"That works." He waited, wondering what she was doing here.

As if she'd read his mind, she said, "I'll be shooting those videos Grandpa mentioned away from the house for a day or two. He recommended we use the ranch truck, when you have it available."

For a second, he thought of offering up Tyler as her assistant, but the burst of possessiveness that hit almost left him reeling. He fought to ignore the sensation. "You need me to help move a cactus or two?"

"Ha-ha. I don't drive, remember?"

"Oh, yeah. Will late afternoon tomorrow suit you?"

"Yes, that'll be fine."

He thought of his plans for the rest of the day. Tried not to think about what Jane might be doing.

Tried not to recall what she had said to him the night of the rehearsal—the thing that seemed to bother her just as much as the kids not seeing Marina. Her words had come back to him more than once since that night.

Socializing only with everyone here on the ranch isn't doing you any good. More important, it's keeping your kids from making friends.

Who said he didn't socialize? Going for ice cream was a social occasion, wasn't it? "I'm taking the kids into town to the Big Dipper later this afternoon. Tyler's coming along. Want to join us?"

She hesitated, and for a moment he hoped she would say no. All too easily, he'd let his pride and his desire for her make him forget his own caution to stay away.

"Do you mind if I invite Andi and the kids, too?"

"Sure. The more the merrier. Rachel will like having her friends along." He almost emphasized his final words. That was all he would need now, to be getting as bad as his father with his pointed remarks.

"Great," Jane said. "Then it's a date."

Not much of one, considering they'd have two adult chaperones and a handful of kids along with them.

On the other hand, considering that caution of his, he ought to be glad for the reinforcements.

JANE LOOKED AT her cousin in dismay.

After breakfast, she had wandered up to Andi's room to tell her about their date for the afternoon, only to discover her cousin had other plans.

She would never have agreed to go out with Pete—and his kids and Tyler, of course—if she had known Andi couldn't come with them. Pete hadn't had to spell things out to her about Tyler. She had seen the man with Shay at the wedding and knew exactly why he was along for the ride.

She had a feeling she knew why *she'd* been invited, too. The thought made her insides turn soft as sun-warmed chocolate. But she couldn't get so close to Pete again. Not until she told him the truth.

"I'm sorry," Andi said, looking genuinely distraught at Jane's dismay. Missy had just finished a bottle, and Andi held her up to her shoulder to burp her. "Dad's not leaving for a couple more days, but now he's living in Florida, he may not see the kids again for a while."

"No, I'm sorry," she said. "I wasn't thinking. Although..." She frowned. "You haven't been talking to Tina, have you?"

Andi looked puzzled. "Not since last night. Why?"

"Oh, nothing."

"Uh-huh. Okay, the chair's over there." She pointed. "Sit."

"What?"

"Sit. And tell me all about what's bugging you."

"Who said anything was?" But she pulled the chair over from the small desk, kicked off her shoes and propped her feet on the edge of Andi's bed.

"Come on, Jane. Remember who you're talking to here."

"Yeah." After their many vacations and holidays together at Garland Ranch, she was probably closer to Andi than any other female she knew.

Though she had already discussed Pete with her, she felt reluctant to bring him into another conversation. And she certainly wouldn't reveal to anyone what he had said about his ex-wife deserting her children.

Again, she wondered what he had wanted to say to her last night. But after the reception, when they'd met outside, she had gotten too distracted to pursue the question…

Fighting to focus now, she slumped back in her seat and sighed. "Rachel has taken a liking to me."

"Yes, I've noticed she always looks for you. I think it's cute."

"Maybe. But I sure don't know much about kids."

"You could learn."

"And isn't that ironic. I'd have to learn what you and Tina were born knowing."

Andi laughed. "Of course we weren't."

"Well, you've got the knack for it, then." She shook her head. "It doesn't matter. I don't have time for kids in my life anyway. But I don't want to do or say the wrong thing with Rachel. And I'm not sure how to handle it."

"Rachel's interest…or Rachel's daddy?"

"Both," she confessed. Briefly, she explained about Pete's reaction to Rachel's makeup for the wedding.

"I can understand that. He's just trying to protect his little girl, and he's probably in over his head."

"You think that's all it is?"

"Of course. I struggle with it, too. It's not easy being a single parent. And sometimes it's not easy being the child of a single parent. I'm probably too overprotective of the kids."

No, Andi wasn't overprotective, just trying to fill the gap left by the parent they had lost. In his own way, wasn't Pete trying to do that, too?

She sighed again.

Andi laughed and shook her head. "Missy," she said lightly to the baby, "Cousin Jane has got it bad."

She sat up straight. "I have not. I just… We just…"

"Wow. I've never seen you at such a loss for words." Andi gasped. "*Jane.* So *that's* why you walked off last night. You slept with Pete."

She groaned. "There's no point in denying it to you, I guess. It wasn't planned, believe me. And it never should have happened. But there's worse." After a long, deep breath, she added, "I've contacted Marina to ask her to be spokesperson for the Hitching Post."

"Oh," Andi said dully. "That's not good."

"I know it. And now I have to tell Pete."

Andi took a deep breath of her own. "Listen. We've heard what Marina is like. Chances are, she won't show."

"I've thought of that." *Hoped for* that.

"Then don't worry about something that may never happen," Andi advised. "Just go. Have fun, eat ice cream. Be someone new for Rachel to talk to while you're here. She needs that, I think. So does Pete. And it will be good for you, too. You'll see I'm right."

WHAT JANE SAW during their visit to the Big Dipper only reinforced her opinion of Pete Brannigan as both a very good father and a smoking-hot man.

Inside the store, Rachel chose one ice-cream flavor after another, immediately changing her mind after each decision. Pete patiently walked her through the entire selection more than once.

Fortunately, there were no other customers lined up behind them yet. Even if there had been, service would have been slow. Shay, the only clerk working, stood chatting with Tyler at the front counter.

Jane spent her time watching Pete. He'd worn a tight green T-shirt that showed off a number of assets, including his hazel-green eyes. He'd also worn a pair of equally tight jeans that could earn him justifiable bragging rights. She ought to know.

"See anything you like?" he asked.

Startled, she looked up. Rachel had wandered back to the first of the ice-cream tubs again. Jane looked across the shop at Eric, happy in his high chair beside a table for four. She rested her hands on the cold metal of the display case and leaned forward.

"They're out of black walnut," she said.

"I could offer you something better," he murmured into her ear.

She laughed. "You do have a good opinion of yourself, don't you, cowboy?"

"I didn't hear you complaining. Or was that what all the moaning meant?"

"Pete!" Despite her chilled palms, he'd gotten her hot all over. And *that* was what had resulted in her pleasurable moans last night.

His laugh stirred the hair near her cheek. He placed his hand at the small of her back, setting off an inferno.

"Daddy," Rachel called, "can I have strawberry *and* chocolate?"

"You know what happened last time you tried to eat so much. How about I have the strawberry and you eat some of it, and you have the chocolate—with sprinkles."

"Yes, I *have* to have sprinkles."

"All right." He leaned closer again. "And you, Jane? What do you *have* to have?"

"I'll think about it." She smiled. "Meanwhile, I'll settle for pistachio."

When they could finally get Shay's attention, they ordered their ice cream, which Tyler insisted was his treat.

"Thank you," Rachel said. "When I get big, I'll have money and then I'll take my turn."

"I'll remember that," Tyler said with a smile.

Jane led the way to the table. When she took a seat, she discovered Tyler had remained at the counter and Rachel had opted for a table for two near the front window.

"I have to look for my friends," she called.

Which left Jane alone with Pete, who sat across from her, put a small cup of ice cream in front of Eric and then looked up at her with a half smile.

"What?" she asked.

"Just thinking about what Rachel said to Tyler. 'Thank you' and a promise to pay him back. Last night at the reception, it was 'sorry' and concern that Sharon and Eric wouldn't get a good seat."

At the tender look on his face, her heart gave a tiny lurch. "Your little girl's growing up."

He leaned over the table and whispered, "And she's finally learning her manners."

She had to struggle to keep her laugh low. Pete shifted

in his chair, accidentally kicking her beneath the table. "Ow. What size boots are you wearing, cowboy?"

"Twelve."

"No wonder you almost broke my toe."

"Sorry."

"So polite," she teased. "Like father, like daughter. You've got manners, too?"

"I try."

"Such as?"

"I held the door when we got here, didn't I? And I opened the door in the truck for you."

"That's true," she admitted. "What else?"

"I always tip my hat to a lady."

"And?"

"And I don't take the last piece of pie on a plate."

"Why not?"

He shrugged. "Because I'd miss out on dessert for the whole next week."

"That's how your dad punished you?"

"We didn't do punishment. That's how he showed he ruled the house. How about yours?"

"Oh, it usually involved a few push-ups or cleaning the latrine." She grinned. "I'd rather do that any day than give up sweets."

"I can believe it. I saw you at the dessert table at the reception." He lowered his voice. "I saw you with those chocolates last night. You're not planning to fit into that dress much longer, are you?"

"Pete Brannigan! I'll have you know I'm a perfect—" She clamped her mouth shut for a moment. "Oh, no, you don't."

"What?"

"You're not getting my dress size."

"Why not? You're into that game of Twenty Questions I didn't want to play last night, aren't you? Starting with my boot size. You ought to give me your dress size, unless you want me checking the next time I take one off you."

She gasped.

His deep laugh thrummed through her. "You're only up to seven, by the way."

"I'm impressed."

"Don't be. Under the table, I'm counting on my fingers. I learned that from Rachel."

She laughed. "Is she good in math?"

"As long as she doesn't have to go above ten. She's better at reading. I've been reading books to her since she was Eric's age."

She could see him with a storybook in his large hands and a little blond-haired girl on his knee. The image brought a lump to her throat. "And what about Eric?"

"No, he hasn't read anything to Rachel yet."

She rolled her eyes. "You know what I mean."

"So far, I've read only the sports stats."

"And only if the numbers are under ten?"

"Yes. That's ten questions. You've just hit the halfway point."

"I can't have."

He pulled his hands out from under the table and held them up, all fingers splayed. Instantly, she recalled him touching her back just that way while they'd danced… and later, touching her in other ways and other places.

Pete rested his hands on the table and locked his gaze with hers.

The door of the shop opened. She heard Rachel squeal. Grateful for being saved from embarrassing herself in public, Jane turned to look.

Carrying her ice-cream dish and spoon in one hand

and tugging a woman across the room with the other, Rachel walked up to the table. "Daddy! Jane! This is Miss Loring."

"I know that, sweetheart," Pete said. "Miss Loring, nice to see you again."

The woman was tall and slim with auburn hair and a stubborn chin. Just the type to teach a class of kindergartners. Just the type to make a perfect mommy?

As he made introductions, Jane smiled. "A pleasure to meet you, Miss Loring. I've heard a lot about you."

"Rachel's told me quite a bit about you, too."

"I did, Jane. I told Miss Loring about dropping the flowers and about the chocolates we ate in the cabin, and I told Miss Loring I asked to take a piece for Robbie."

Miss Loring smiled down at the little girl for a moment, nodded even more fleetingly at Jane, then finally turned to Pete.

"Rachel's deportment has improved considerably in the past couple of weeks, Mr. Brannigan."

"She's excited about graduating and moving up to the grade school."

"It's more than that. I think she's had some new good influence in her life." She glanced toward Jane and smiled again. Then she turned to Rachel. "I'll see you in class tomorrow."

Rachel nodded energetically. "Okay, Miss Loring. And I won't need any time-outs."

The three adults laughed. Miss Loring left to go to the counter, and Rachel turned to Pete.

"I'm ready for more." She looked down at his dish. "Daddy! What happened to your ice cream? It's a puddle."

He winked at Jane, then looked soberly at his daughter. "Rachel, haven't you ever heard of strawberry soup?"

Shaking her head, Jane laughed. She'd been right.

Pete was both a very good father and a smoking-hot man.

And now one heck of a fun date.

Chapter Fifteen

After supper at the Hitching Post, Jane went to the cabin again. Partly because she wanted to finish up the photos and partly because she wanted to destroy evidence of what had happened here last night—the candy wrappers, the pile of pillows. The unmade bed. The proof she and Pete had...had been together.

The door opened, and as if her memory of him had brought him to her, Pete walked into the cabin.

"I saw the light and thought it might be you here." He set a plastic bag on the coffee table and moved toward her.

Her heart skipped a beat. She had almost hoped they wouldn't find a chance to be together on their own again. "I thought I'd get a few more photos in." Turning back to her scene, she focused on the camera, trying to be strong, trying to remember just why she needed to keep her distance. "I want to wrap things up in here."

"Sure about that?"

She jumped. He now spoke from directly behind her. "You move quietly in those size-twelves, cowboy."

"I'm good when I want to be."

He'd moved in again, so close his breath stirred her hair. His chest brushed against her back. Whatever was about to happen, she could choose to end it right now. She could walk away. She could ask him to leave.

She turned and murmured, "How good *can* you be?"

In the flickering light from the candles she had lit, his eyes glowed. Gently, he lifted the strap from around her neck and set the camera on the counter beside the bag. She held her breath, wanting to run…and just wanting.

"Since we ate all the chocolates last night," he said, "I brought you a surprise."

"Really? What?"

He opened the bag and, with a flourish, pulled out a quart of black-walnut ice cream.

She laughed, her eyes misting. "You do know how to seduce a girl, don't you?"

"I can try."

"But I thought the Big Dipper was out of black walnut."

"This is imported from the next town over."

"You really went above and beyond, then. Thank you." She looked at the carton. "Is it soup yet?"

"Nope. I've got it on ice. Which means it can wait." He set the container back in the bag. "We'll have it for dessert."

He returned to her side and kissed her.

Long minutes later, when at last they were lying atop the pristine white sheets again, he began to do other things. Things that made her heart pound and her pulse race and her eyes prickle from imminent tears.

She thought of all the truths she could finally admit to herself and the one truth she didn't want to face.

She loved this loving daddy, this fun date.

She loved this champion and protector.

She loved this thoroughly hot man.

And tomorrow she would have to tell him she had invited his ex-wife back to Cowboy Creek.

She felt sure she knew how he would react to the news. But she refused to let that thought spoil her time with him tonight.

AS HE WATCHED Jane savor the last of the melted ice cream, Pete stifled a groan.

He'd had a good time—a *great* time—at the Big Dipper with her and the kids. What had started off as a need to get her out of his system…what had turned them into lovers…had begun to feel like something else. Like they could be friends. Like they could be more than friends.

He deserved to kick himself for those thoughts. His kids had to come first.

By the time he'd gotten Rachel into bed tonight, he knew he'd let her in for even more heartbreak. She could talk of nothing but ice cream—and Jane.

He could think of nothing but Jane.

The ice cream he'd brought now was incidental. A seduction, she had called it, but he hadn't planned it that way. He hadn't meant to wind up in bed with her again. Yet when he'd seen her standing in the flickering candlelight with the bed right behind her, he hadn't been able to keep from giving in.

He'd wanted his mouth on hers again. He'd needed to kiss her. And more.

"You're quiet," she said.

"Just resting. You wore me out." Then she gave him that low, sexy laugh. As always, the sound made him want to move closer. Instead of giving in to his cravings, he ought to be running as fast and as far as he could.

"How's the black-walnut soup?" he asked.

"Delicious. You sure you don't want some?"

"No, thanks."

"Then have another chocolate. I found it under the

pillow." She unwrapped the foil and fed him the small square.

He took her wrist, kissed her palm and closed her fingers into a fist.

"What was that for?"

"Just felt like it." He wasn't about to volunteer anything so sappy as *It's something for you to remember me by when you leave*. But he thought it. The look on her face made him wonder if she'd caught on.

"I should get dressed," she said. "I need..."

"I need, too." He skimmed his hand up her flat, bare belly and leaned over to kiss her ice-cream-cooled mouth. She rose to dress again and he lay watching, hoping for the pleasure of taking those clothes off her again. He could get used to this.

And that was just the problem.

He *couldn't* get used to this.

Jane took a seat on one of the stools at the breakfast counter, then pushed aside the bag from the ice cream Pete had used to seduce her. Not that she had needed much of a bribe.

Walking away from that man—that hot, naked, oh-so-touchable man—was the hardest thing she had ever done. She shouldn't have let him sway her, yet after her certainty that last night would be their only time together, tonight had seemed a gift.

At last, she turned back to him. He had dressed again and stood fastening the button on his jeans.

"Pete, we have to talk."

He sighed. "I know we do. That was the plan yesterday, but things got out of hand." He came to stand on the other side of the breakfast counter. "I want to talk to you about Marina."

She held her breath. She had to talk to him about his

ex-wife, too—no matter how much she wished she could forget all about the woman.

She had hoped to help a little girl who missed her mother, had intended to help Pete understand his daughter's feelings. She hadn't expected to hear the story of Pete's marriage and divorce.

And she definitely didn't want to hear the pain in his voice.

Did he still hurt that much from what his ex-wife had done years ago? Or did he still feel that pain because he hadn't stopped caring about the woman he'd once married?

"I know you're not one for kids," he said, "so this might be too much information, but you need to know what I was dealing with when it came to my ex." He half turned to rest his hip against the counter.

She couldn't see his eyes now, only part of his profile, the strong line of his jaw, the tension-revealing tic of muscle marring the flat plane of his cheek.

"When Marina first left, Sharon and I got Eric through the worst of it. By the time she dropped in for a visit, I think he'd forgotten her. No, I prayed he'd forgotten." She had to strain to hear his voice. "Marina didn't have much interest at all in seeing him. As for Rachel..." His jaw softened with his small smile. "You know my daughter. She's always been a hard one to avoid."

He stayed silent for a few moments. She could see a vein in his neck pulsing. He clenched his hands as he knotted his fingers together. Finally, he sighed. "It was hard for her to accept that her mama was here for her one day, then gone the next."

She reached across the counter to squeeze his arm. He didn't look up, didn't acknowledge her touch, but his fingers relaxed slightly.

"That's about what Marina's visits added up to," he continued. "She'd breeze through town, stay as short a time as she could and leave again."

"Why did she bother coming back?"

"Beats me. The visits got more and more erratic, and every time she left, Rachel got more and more upset." He shook his head. "When Marina came to town, she made a big splash, brought presents for Rachel and Eric, threw cash around town like it was play money from a kid's game."

He moved to stand by the suite's small sink, bracing his hands on the edge, keeping his back turned to her. "Marina had money, fame, trips to Paris for her fashion shows, a big house in California. All things she got from her new modeling career."

"It must have been a strong lure."

The look he shot her made her heart ache.

"Marina didn't need much of a lure. That's what she had always wanted. It was never anything that appealed to me. I don't need the lifestyle, the fame, the money. And my kids don't need any of that, either." He shrugged and added simply, "We're a family. We just need each other."

Nervous tension made her stomach spasm. What was he going to think when he found out what she had done?

"After the divorce went through," he said, "and Marina stopped coming to town at all, it was a blessing in disguise. Hell, it was an outright answer to prayer." He turned to face her. "Now, you see why I'm not so keen on having my ex around?"

She swallowed hard. "I didn't know."

"I realize that. That's why I've filled you in."

Her heart sank. This very private man had opened up to her, had told her things he hadn't shared even with her family. And now she had to confess.

"Pete, I'm sorry."

"No harm done."

"I'm afraid there might be."

He frowned.

She forced herself not to look away. "I didn't know anything about Marina, just about what Rachel said and how she seemed to feel. I only wanted to help her. And Eric. And you. I hope you believe that."

He nodded. "Now drop the other shoe."

She took a deep breath and admitted, "I've already contacted Marina."

"You...?" He shook his head as if in denial. As if in disbelief at her stupidity. "You did *what*?"

"I got in touch with Marina. About being the spokesperson for the hotel. I haven't heard a word back. And considering what you've told me, it's probably unlikely she'll agree to come here."

He muttered a curse. "You contacted her—after I'd told you that idea wouldn't work? After all I'd said about her, about how she disappointed the kids? What were you thinking?"

"I told you. I wanted to help."

"Yeah? By going over my head. Interfering with my family. And doing the one thing that will hurt Rachel most. That might be your idea of help, but it sure as hell isn't mine."

Chapter Sixteen

Four days later, Jane followed her family into the Cowboy Creek Elementary School auditorium.

She hadn't seen Pete since he had stormed out of the cabin Sunday night. She had seen Rachel when the little girl came in search of her, which was often.

"You *have* to be at my graduation, Jane," Rachel had reminded her. "Don't forget."

"I won't," she promised. It was a promise she had kept, though now a small part of her regretted it. The look on Pete's face when he'd seen her outside in the parking lot just now had left her numb.

Inside, her family had begun filing into a row of seats. At the front of the room, what sounded like three hundred children ran around behind the curtain-covered stage, while two harried voices rose in an attempt to regain order.

Jane spotted Miss Loring near the floor space blocked off for an orchestra pit. Students tuned their instruments, adding to the noise from behind the curtain.

When Miss Loring looked her way, Jane gave her a wave and a sympathetic smile. The teacher smiled back, as unruffled as Rachel had been during her walk down the aisle.

Thanks to the rehearsal. Thanks to her.

As she had told Pete, all she had wanted to do was help. She winced at the memory of his snapped response.

"Jane," Jed called, "are you planning to join us?"

Startled, she turned to find her family had taken their seats. Sharon and Eric had joined the Garlands. Sugar Conway was there, too.

Pete was sitting one seat over from the aisle.

Jed beamed at her. "We left you a place at the end. So you could take all your pictures."

"Thanks, Grandpa." She slipped into the vacant space beside Pete. She could smell his aftershave, a subtle but potent mixture of musk and spice. When she settled back, his broad shoulder brushed hers, sending ripples of warmth to her elbow, reminding her of the way he'd touched her arms and her back and her neck, all exposed by her halter-top gown.

Stopping the memories right there, she clung to her camera, telling herself she needed to pay attention to what she was doing. The camera was a valuable piece of equipment, and if she dropped it, it would break.

The parallel made her wince again. Pete had already dropped her, and her heart felt broken.

Everyone around them was talking. He sat silent, staring ahead at the curtain-covered stage. Maybe from another audience member's perspective, he would look like an anxious dad, but sitting this close beside him, she saw the telltale tic in his cheek.

It hurt to think she might have caused it.

Her only consolation was she'd never heard back from his wife.

She struggled to find something to say. The first question she could come up with stemmed from her own emotions. "Was Rachel nervous on the way into town?"

"No. She was busy telling us about the seating arrangements for tonight."

"Tonight?" She looked at him. Had Rachel arranged for them to sit together?

"She wanted us to take places at the front of the room."

As the curtains began to part, she settled back in her seat. Pete leaned forward slightly, probably eager to get his first look at his daughter. Or to move away from her.

Jane's palms grew a little damp as she thought about Rachel's big moment.

The curtains swung open. By some miracle, the teachers had gathered the students into three straight rows. Rachel, one of the shortest of them, stood in the center of the front row.

Once, she could only have imagined how Pete would have felt at this moment. Now she knew.

Rachel grinned at Jed and Pete and Jane.

Jane smiled back, her broken heart swelling with pride.

AS HE PARKED his truck outside SugarPie's after his daughter's graduation, Pete was still kicking himself.

For the past few days, he'd gotten Tyler to substitute for him on Jane's excursions for her scenic videos. As he'd told Tyler, she didn't need anyone to move scenery, and the other man could operate the truck just as well as he could.

Yesterday, Jed had come to the barn and casually mentioned Jane had finished her videos. He'd already known that through Tyler, but he was relieved Jed knew it, too. That let him off the hook for any more jobs as Jane's assistant.

He would have to worry about Marina's appearance when—and if—it happened. He'd heard nothing yet about her responding to Jane's message, and if everything went as usual with his ex-wife, he wouldn't have to deal with her at all.

"Daddy!" Rachel called from the backseat of the truck, bouncing as much as she could, considering she wore a snug seat belt. "Did you see me up on the stage?"

"I sure did, sweetheart."

"Did Jane take my picture?"

"Yes, she did." She—along with all the parents and grandparents in the audience—had taken quite a few.

He went around the truck to open Sharon's door, which brought back the memory of Jane asking him about his manners. He hadn't shown much politeness to her the last night they'd been together. Since then, he hadn't seen her at all.

Until this evening.

He had spotted the ranch's SUV pulling into the school parking lot, followed by Cole's truck. Jed and Paz and Andi and her kids had all come to Rachel's graduation. Even the newlyweds and Robbie had arrived home just in time.

When he'd seen Jane, his heart had sunk. Rachel didn't need the memory of having the woman there on her special night, but with Jed's entire family along, he couldn't argue.

When Jed had asked him to leave the aisle seat open for Jane, he hadn't protested.

And when she'd sat beside him, smelling of vanilla and spice, he'd nearly lost the control he'd fought so hard to hang on to.

Now he waved to the Garlands before ushering Sharon and the kids into the sandwich shop. Rachel's squeal of pleasure when she saw all the balloons and streamers on one side of the room took his mind from Jane... for a little while.

"Well, here's our graduate," Sugar said. A solid, gray-haired woman, she had a surprisingly gentle Southern drawl. "Rachel, I believe you look just like a first-grade girl now."

"I *am* a first-grade girl, Sugar—look!" Proudly, she displayed her diploma.

"Very nice. I'll just take that and put it up on the cupboard here so you don't get it dirty while you're eating."

The shop door opened again. "Jane!" Rachel waved. "Come here and sit by me! Please!"

"Rachel, maybe Jane would like to choose her own seat."

"Oh, no, Daddy. I get to tell everybody where to sit because it's my party. Just like the wedding."

"I would say the girl's got that right." Jed beamed at her.

"I agree." Jane took her designated seat at the largest of the round tables SugarPie's had available.

The table wasn't big enough to fit their group comfortably, but everyone agreed with Rachel that it was nice to sit together. Good thing they were all there only for dessert and drinks, or half the group could easily have worn supper in their laps.

By the time she had completed the arrangements to her satisfaction, Pete found himself wedged between Jane and Jed again, and again, he found his control slipping.

"'Scuse me." Jed shifted his chair to allow Paz more room.

Pete did the same for Jed, which put him closer to Jane. He gave thanks they were at SugarPie's. The kitchen always filled the bakery and sandwich shop with the aromas of cinnamon and spices. That helped distract him from the scent of Jane's perfume.

He couldn't do much about her nearness, though. As

Jed shifted his chair again, Pete was forced to slide his over. His shoulder bumped Jane's. It was the auditorium all over again.

"Sorry," he said.

"It's a tight squeeze, isn't it?" she said coolly.

"Yeah. And there's no way we can sit like sardines and not rub shoulders." He rested against his seat and stretched his arm along the top of her chair. He would just have to eat his cake one-handed and as a temporary southpaw. "That better?"

"It's fine."

On Rachel's other side, Sharon sat holding Eric, who strained forward, his arms held toward Jane.

"That means you have to hold him," Rachel said.

"Sugar's bringing a high chair," Pete told her.

"But Eric wants to see Jane."

"I don't mind," Jane said.

Pete rose to reach across the table for his son, then placed him in Jane's lap. She was back to wearing her basic black, along with her silver jewelry. Eric immediately grabbed her waist-length rope necklace and tugged.

"Eric." Pete reached for one of his fists.

"It's only costume jewelry," Jane said. "Don't worry about it."

Even as she spoke, his son made a grab for one of her dangling silver earrings. Jane gave a muffled grunt of pain.

Pete lunged, immobilizing Eric's hand and then uncurling his fingers.

"Just take them off, please," she said.

Even after all they had done together in the cabin, it felt oddly intimate to touch her earrings and slip their long hooks from her earlobes. He pocketed the pair and made a mental note to return them to her before they left

SugarPie's. "You're going to be in for a real challenge when Layne serves the ice cream and cake."

"Maybe I'll skip it, then. I might want to wear my blue dress again soon."

He registered the dig at him but didn't acknowledge it.

The longer he watched Eric cling to Jane and listened to Rachel chat excitedly with her, the more his heart sank. The kids were too darned attached to her—literally, in Eric's case.

"Jane, did you see my diploma already?" Rachel asked.

"Yes, and I got some pictures of you when Miss Loring handed it to you on the stage."

"Can we give one to Miss Loring? Please? She's going to miss me when I leave her class. She told me."

"I'm sure she *will* miss you."

"But I'm going to be a first-grader next year. Did you know that?"

"Yes, I did. You'll have lots of fun in grade school, and you'll learn a lot, too."

"Good. One of these days, I have to count better past ten."

"You'll get there. I wasn't good at math when I was in kindergarten, either."

"Really?"

"Really. I'll tell you a secret. I could never remember which came first, six or seven."

"Wow. I can remember that. Maybe I *will* get better, like Daddy says."

"Of course you will," Pete assured her.

"You're getting better already," Sharon said.

After Sugar brought the high chair for Eric, there was a lull in the conversation, punctuated only by his son's screech when Jane attempted to transfer him to his new seat.

As Pete reached over to uncurl Eric's fingers from her

necklace again, his own hands brushed Jane's blouse. "Sorry," he muttered.

This time, she didn't respond to his apology, coolly or otherwise.

Finally, they had Eric detangled and deposited—just in the nick of time, as Layne had arrived with a tray filled with their dessert.

Pete spooned up a mouthful of ice cream. "Nice not to have soup for a change, isn't it?"

Jane nodded.

He might as well give up. He didn't know why he was trying anyhow, except for the sake of politeness. After all, he had to keep setting a good example for Rachel.

After his daughter had made serious inroads on her dessert, she looked around the table. "Pretty soon, I'm going to have my first day of first-grade school."

"After the summer's over, I think," said Andi.

"Yes. Jane, on the first day, will you take me to school?"

A beat went by, then a second and a third. Finally, Jane said, "I don't drive, Rachel."

She didn't say *I won't be here*. But he knew that was the truth. Just like his ex-wife, Jane wouldn't be there for his kids. At least, he had to give her credit for not wanting to burst Rachel's bubble at her own graduation party.

"Then Daddy can drive me. Right, Daddy?"

"Right, sweetheart. Anything for you. If Grandpa Jed will give me that morning off, that is."

Everyone laughed.

"You know," Jed said, "I think it's about time we had a toast."

"But it's not the wedding," Rachel said.

"I know, but we're celebrating, and I think we ought to raise a toast to you."

"To *me*?" Her mouth dropped open.

"Yes. Pete, you'll do the honors?"

"Of course." Pete held up his iced-tea glass and waited for everyone to follow suit. "To Rachel, my number one best girl. We're all very proud of you for graduating from kindergarten."

"Hear, hear," said Jed.

When Rachel reached her glass in Pete's direction, he leaned forward past Jane to meet her.

This close, he couldn't help picking up the scent of Jane's perfume. This close, his chin brushed her soft, black hair. Sternly, he ignored the assault to his senses.

He focused instead on his daughter, one of the two wonders of his world. A world that could never include Jane Garland.

JANE HAD TAKEN all the photos of the hotel she would need, had shot all the video footage she wanted. It was time for her to get back to the real world.

Her world.

Pete's absence earlier that week had made it clear she didn't need to hang around for him. He'd gone from fun and charming at the ice-cream parlor to cold as ice when he'd simply told Tyler to let her know he instead of Pete would take her on the tour of the ranch.

Yet, despite the fact the fun with Pete was over and she was eager to resume her hard-earned career, she felt reluctant to leave.

She wondered if her time in Cowboy Creek was showing her just what her life was missing.

Time to relax. Time to work on photos for her portfolio. Time to spend with her family and Paz and Rachel. All that had come together for her at the rehearsal dinner and the wedding, at Rachel's graduation yesterday, and then later at the party at SugarPie's.

But she couldn't have all that.

She wouldn't have her own world again for a while now, either, thanks to what she had just found in her cell phone inbox. She had been thumbing through texts and email, which she hadn't checked the day before.

She sat on the front porch and, between reading messages, watched the sun come up over a range of pine-tree-covered mountains. Stark green against bold yellow made a striking contrast, but it was an indication of her mood that she didn't reach for the camera on the swing beside her.

When was the last time she had seen a sunrise that wasn't from her seat on an airplane? Or from a taxi headed to an airport's departure gates?

She heard a clop-clop sound on the hard-packed earth coming from somewhere close by, something she never had the opportunity to notice in her own world unless her taxi happened to cut through Central Park. She hadn't even ridden a horse in years, not even gentle old Daffodil, and here she was, growing nostalgic over the sound of a horse's approach.

The clopping sound grew louder. She shifted on the swing to look toward the driveway. A moment later, Pete, astride a huge black horse, appeared from around the side of the hotel. One glance at him stole her breath.

From his Stetson down to his boots, he looked every inch the man he wanted to be—so much more than just a cowboy who preferred a simple life. She saw a rancher who clung with pride to old-fashioned values. A man who loved horses and living close to the land. A daddy who would do anything to protect his kids.

Every single one of those traits made him exactly the wrong man for her. Why did she still find him so darned attractive?

Worse, how could she have let him break her heart?

No doubt about it. She definitely needed to get back to her own world.

She watched Pete swing himself from the horse and loop the reins over the railing.

She glanced down at her camera as he climbed the steps, his size-twelve boots shattering the silence.

"Morning," he said.

She nodded and continued to scroll.

He reached out and dropped the earrings she'd worn to the graduation in her lap. "Forgot to give these to you last night."

"Yes. I thought of them later on."

"I'd have come by once we got home, but it took Rachel a while to settle down and then get to sleep."

She wasn't the only one. "I'm not surprised. She was pretty keyed up at SugarPie's."

"And the sugar didn't help."

"No. And Eric?" What was she doing, chatting about his kids as if she did it every day? As if she would recognize anything that had upset them or thrown them off their routines? As if he would care that she cared enough to ask about them?

"Out like a light on the way home in the truck. Sharon changed him and put him to bed, and he didn't wake up once."

"That's good."

"Jed says Andi and the kids are going home today."

"Yes."

"I'll send Rachel over to say goodbye."

She nodded.

"And you?"

"Am I leaving? No, not yet." She scrolled down the

screen of her cell phone, clicked a button and handed him the phone.

He glanced down, then returned it to her. "So she's coming to town."

"Looks like it."

"When did you find out?"

"Just a few minutes ago, when I read that message."

He nodded, and that was that.

But as he began to turn away, she saw his expression. The quick glimpse told her everything he hadn't said. *She* was the cause of his unhappiness and confusion.

The knowledge filled her with guilt and regret.

JANE HADN'T EXPECTED to see Pete again soon, but he came with Rachel to say farewell to Andi and her children.

She was happy to have gained a spokesperson for the Hitching Post. Yet ever since that morning, when she had received Marina's message and shared the news of his wife's return with Pete, she had been fighting mixed emotions of her own.

"Pull up some chairs, you two," Jed insisted. "You've got to have a piece of Paz's cheesecake."

When Pete said he needed to get back to the house, she debated following him. But then Rachel claimed a seat beside her and said, "Guess what, everybody. My mama's coming to visit me!"

A stunned silence fell over the room, until Jane smiled and said, "That's great news, Rachel."

With the little girl's announcement, the worries Jane had fought all day flooded over her. "Excuse me," she said, rising. "I'll be back in just a few minutes."

"I'll save your seat for you, Jane," Rachel said.

"Thank you." She walked casually from the room. The minute she cleared the dining room doorway, she rushed down the hallway, hoping she was in time to catch Pete before he reached home or entered the barn.

Her feet must have flown, because when she burst through the hotel's front door, she found him still on the porch. She almost skidded to a halt in her effort to avoid bumping into him.

"I'm…glad I caught you," she said. "This morning when we spoke, I was still only half-awake. But I have to admit, when you showed up, I was also still stunned after reading Marina's message."

"Were you?" he asked. Unlike the last time they'd met, she couldn't read his expression. In his flat tone, she couldn't find anything to relieve her guilt.

His reaction to the message from his wife had bothered her the entire day. That wasn't the only thing that upset her.

The twinge of unease she felt over Rachel's eagerness to see her mother was half the problem. The other half was discomfort at the thought of Pete's ex returning to town.

Unease. Discomfort. Such bland words to describe what she didn't want to feel. Could she really be jealous of Rachel's need to see her mother again or envious of the attraction Marina still held for her children?

If so, what kind of person did that make her?

"You told Rachel about Marina?" she asked Pete.

"She overheard me telling Sharon."

"Oh. Well, after you left the dining room, Rachel mentioned it to everyone. She seems very happy about it."

"Yeah. She's already shared her feeling with us. A few times."

She hesitated, then said, "Isn't it good that she still wants to see Marina?" She wanted to reassure herself as much as she hoped to convince him.

He looked out toward the same mountain range she had scrutinized that morning. Now the sun's slanting rays showcased those deep green pines below a blue sky filled with puffy white clouds. He stared awhile before turning to look at her again.

"I guess, no matter what, Marina is still my kids' mama."

"That's what I've been trying to say all along. She *is* their mother—even if, from what you tell me, she doesn't act like it. Maybe eventually, she will. I hope she makes the effort to have a relationship with the kids. And with you, if that's what you want."

For a moment, she thought she might have pushed too far in trying to find out how much damage she had done. But she had to know. She felt relieved to realize she'd meant what she said. She truly *did* hope Marina's return would work out for the best. But she couldn't forget the memory of Pete's confusion and pain.

"Don't get me wrong," he said. "My ex is just…" He paused, sighed and gestured toward the mountains. "She's about as reliable and substantial as those clouds. She always has been flighty, flaky and—first and above all—concerned about herself."

While *his* first concern would always be his children.

The thought made her heart swell just a bit.

"So now you know the big deal about why I objected when you wanted to do an entire photo shoot with Rachel. Or, on second thought, maybe you still don't."

When he strode away, she sank onto the porch swing.

There was something wrong there, something else he hadn't told her. She knew it.

But she also knew now his reluctance to communicate with her was only an effort to mask his worry for his kids. To care for them and to keep them from getting hurt.

The knowledge made her care even more about him.

And that made it even more important for her to keep her distance.

Chapter Seventeen

Jane hadn't moved from the porch swing when her phone vibrated with a new message. It was from Marina, letting her know the limousine had arrived at the Hitching Post from the airport.

She had seen Pete cross the yard and enter his own house, and for that, she felt immensely grateful. On her own behalf, because she wouldn't have to witness his reunion with Marina. And on his, because he wouldn't have to see Rachel's ecstatic reaction to finally being with her mother again.

She entered the hotel and followed the voices to the sitting room off the lobby. Almost everyone was there.

No one noticed her at first, and she spent a moment observing Marina.

She had to admit the woman was everything her photographer friend had reported from that Paris runway and more—tall, slim, with the stunning green eyes and wavy blond hair she had passed down to her children. As a woman, Jane felt a flash of envy. As a photographer, she could only admire the model's photogenic perfection and respect the hard work that went hand in hand with her profession.

When she saw the mounds of torn wrapping paper and the presents piled between Marina and Rachel on the couch, her heart sank. Pete had said his ex-wife always showed up bearing gifts—and then left soon after. But maybe the woman had changed. For her children's sake, Jane hoped so.

When Rachel saw her in the doorway, she shrieked, "Jane—look! This is my mama!"

Obviously, the little girl was over-the-moon excited.

"I thought so," Jane said. "Marina, nice to meet you. As I said in my email, I'm so glad you were willing to be our spokesperson and could fit this shooting into your schedule."

"My pleasure."

"Look what Mama brought me!" Proudly, Rachel held up one gift after another, skirts and dresses and pajamas, a doll, several games.

"Very nice, Rachel," Jane told her.

"And I have more for Eric," Marina assured her daughter.

"You'll stay to lunch, won't you?" Jed asked. "You and Jane can get together afterwards to see about the photos."

"Oh, I'd like to—" she glanced at her watch "—but I'm due in town. I promised some of my local fans I'd meet them at the Cantina. In fact, the limo's still waiting. I'd better go over to the house to see Eric now."

"Can I go with you for lunch, Mama?"

Marina shook her head. "Sorry, honey. That's for grown-ups only."

At the tears in Rachel's eyes, Jane's heart took another dip. The woman had been here all of twenty minutes and had already made other plans. How could she go off and leave her daughter and son so soon?

"You can have lunch here with us, Rachel," Jane said.

But the girl's down-turned mouth showed how little that idea pleased her. "I'll take Mama to see Eric now."

Jane nodded silently, feeling as though she had been demoted in Rachel's eyes. She could handle that. Of course the child would prefer to be with her mother.

What she couldn't handle was the sudden rush of an unnamed emotion connecting her to Rachel and Eric. Compassion? Tenderness? Motherly instincts she had never realized she had?

She already knew how she felt about Pete. But this indefinable emotion made her realize just how much she had come to care for his children, too.

She glanced at Marina and felt as displeased as Rachel had looked just a moment ago.

JANE CHECKED THE natural lighting in the hotel suite and readjusted the vase of flowers she had picked up in town yesterday afternoon. She tried to ignore her growing feeling of irritation. If her spokesperson didn't show up soon, all her efforts would have been wasted. She would have to start today's shoot in a different location.

Marina had taken Jed up on his offer of a room at the Hitching Post, the only hotel within a hundred-mile radius of Cowboy Creek. While she had the limo on call, it only made sense for her to stay here, where she could be just a few hundred yards away from her kids and handy for the photo shoot.

Footsteps on the hallway floor brought her to attention. They weren't Jed's steps. Or Cole's. She knew very well who was walking down the hallway.

Pete came to the door and stood looking around the room as if searching for someone. "Have you seen Marina today?"

"Not yet. I think she may have wanted to sleep in."

"You don't need to cover for her. I saw the limo bring her back after three this morning."

Which meant he hadn't been sleeping, either.

Did that mean he had been watching for Marina?

Her stomach twisted at the thought. Still, her heart went out to him. His ex-wife had arrived only the day before, and already he looked years older.

He prowled the suite as if she might have hidden Marina somewhere in it.

The fact he'd come here this morning when he should have been working made her want to weep. But she pushed her own feelings aside and focused on what was most important. As she had tossed and turned all night, she had thought of Pete and of Rachel and Eric.

"How are the kids?"

"How do you think?" he snapped. "Eric's not sure what's going on, except that he's got a pile of new toys he's too young to play with and a pile of new clothes he's too big to wear."

She didn't want to make excuses for the woman, but she couldn't take seeing Pete this upset. "It would be hard for Marina to know what to buy since..." Since she hadn't seen her children in a year.

"You don't need to cover for her again. She's going to have to face up to this herself, for a change. Rachel's at home, standing just inside the front door and waiting for the bell to ring, because she's sure her mama's going to come calling at any minute."

She winced. "Did Marina come back at all to see them yesterday?"

"No. As usual, she dropped her packages and ran."

"Do you want me to give you a call when I see her?"

"I'll be out working in the western pastures and won't be in again until this afternoon." He sounded almost relieved at having a reason to get away. "Sharon's planning to call over here if she hasn't seen Marina by noon."

It was ten thirty now. "We were supposed to meet here at nine thirty," she admitted. "After breakfast. But she hasn't been downstairs at all yet today."

"She never did like keeping early hours."

Looking away, she said, "If I see Marina before noon, I'll call Sharon myself. I'm sorry about all this."

"Not as sorry as I am." He turned and left the room.

His boots rang out in the hallway again, the sound now twice as loud and quick as before.

Sighing, she set her camera on the desk in one corner of the room.

She couldn't have said how long she had stood staring unseeingly thorough the window before Tina found her there.

Her cousin came into the room and closed the door behind her. She took a seat in the desk chair and went right to the point with a question Jane didn't want to answer. "Did you see Pete?"

Tina's directness showed how unhappy she was with the situation, too.

"Yes," she said reluctantly. "He was here…I don't know how long ago."

Tina frowned. "It couldn't have been more than five minutes. I was in my office when he went past the reception desk without even a wave, and I'd barely gotten my spreadsheet open when he stormed through the lobby and out the door again. Did he talk to Marina?"

"I don't think so. He was here with me for a few minutes."

"Then he couldn't have had the time." Tina sighed. "Jane, I hate to say this, but I don't think inviting Marina here was such a good decision, after all. I wish I hadn't encouraged you."

"Don't worry about it," she said dully. "I thought it

was such a great idea, I would have gone ahead with it regardless."

"I'm so sorry Pete and the kids are having to deal with this."

"Not as sorry as I am." Her eyes prickled as she realized she had repeated Pete's final words to her.

"I could invite Rachel over to play with Robbie today. You know she's here half the time anyway. And then she might get to see more of Marina."

"*None* of us will get to see much of Marina if she spends all her time in town." She shook her head. "Let me take care of it. I'm going to have to say something to her myself."

"Do you think you ought to get any more involved?"

"I can't get any more wrapped up in this than I am already," she admitted.

Tina's dark brown eyes met hers in silent and sympathetic understanding.

JANE COULDN'T HAVE any luck at all talking to Marina when the woman had nine-tenths of her focus on her cell phone.

Not long after Tina left, Marina had shown up in the suite, apologizing profusely and claiming to be ready to get to work. But during the half hour they had been together, the phone had rung or beeped almost continually.

Jane hadn't been able to take even a handful of shots yet.

"Sorry," Marina said, disconnecting the current phone call and evidently switching to text or email, as her thumbs began flying over the keypad. "What were you saying?"

"I was wondering about your schedule and—"

"That's exactly what I'm trying to firm up. My agent's handling a new contract for me—highly confidential. I can't tell you a thing about the assignment, sorry—and we're at a critical stage in the negotiations. I'm expecting something to break any minute." Her keying done, she looked up again.

"When I mentioned schedule, I meant for the time you'll be here in Cowboy Creek."

"I can't stay long," she said in alarm. "I did tell you that in the email?"

"Yes, but—"

"It's been a great visit already. I've been out of touch with my fans here, and it's so good to reconnect."

"With your fans."

"Yes."

"What about your family?"

"I don't have family here anymore." At Jane's startled expression, she added, "Oh, of course, you mean the kids. I've seen Rachel and Eric. I'll touch base with them again, too. But—" Her phone beeped. "My agent. Hold that thought."

Jane bit back her response.

She thought of all the minutes she had logged on her cell phone. Had she ever come across as that rude and self-centered? No wonder Pete had concerns about Rachel craving attention.

She thought of yesterday morning, when he had found her on the front porch and she'd sat scrolling through her email. To her shame, she recalled she had done that deliberately to avoid having to look up at him.

Now she would give anything to be able to meet his eyes without seeing the anger that had filled them when he'd stood in this room a short while ago.

No. At this point, she would give anything just to turn back the clock to last week.

"I've got to go," Marina said abruptly.

"Fine. It's almost noon anyhow. Why don't we get together again after lunch?"

"No, I mean I have to go, as in leave. My agent came through for me, and I need to be back in New York tonight."

"And our photo shoot?"

"I'm sorry. This contract is a very big deal for me…"

And your little website isn't. She could almost hear the words.

"I was happy to do you the favor when I was between commitments," Marina continued. "But now I'm not free. Look, you're a professional, too, Jane. You know what it's like. I've really got to run."

And she did, literally, without giving Jane the chance to say another word.

"SHE'S *WHAT*?"

"Gone."

"What do you mean, *gone*?"

Jane took a deep breath. She had known Pete would be upset.

All afternoon, she had watched the barn from the back porch, waiting to catch him as soon as he returned, hoping she could be the one to break the news about Marina. She owed him that.

Obviously, she had been the first to get to him. But Pete wasn't upset or even angry. He was livid.

"She had to go back to New York for an assignment," she explained. "She left for the airport around noon."

He slammed his fist down so hard on the corral rail, she expected to see a dent in the wood.

"She talk to Rachel and Eric before she left?" he asked.

"No," she said quietly. "She needed to be out of here in fifteen minutes. She was like a madwoman, trying to pack and text and make phone calls, all at once. It wouldn't have been a good time to bring the kids over here."

"'A good time'?" He laughed shortly. "The only time that's good with Marina is the one Marina chooses. I told you that. And again, she breezes in and out and leaves my kids traumatized."

"I'm sorry, Pete. I don't know how many times I can say that. I blame myself—"

"Then we're even," he snapped. "I blame you, too."

She blinked back a sudden rush of tears. She had no idea whether they stemmed from grief or anger or both. "All right, I can understand that. But please, can't we get past the fact I brought her here? We both need to think about the kids. I'll explain to Rachel—"

"No, you won't." He began to pace along the length of the corral fence. "You won't say a thing to her. In fact, you'll stay away from her altogether. Let me do my own damage control."

She nodded. "Of course. Tomorrow, then, I'll talk to her after you've—"

"No." Frowning, he stopped in his tracks. "I just said, stay away from her. Today. Tomorrow. Next week."

She swallowed hard. "But…I'll be leaving soon, too."

"Exactly. To head back to your career, the way Marina flies back to hers."

"Pete—"

He flung up his hand to cut her off. "Just stay away. From all of us."

Without another word, he turned on his heel, then stalked into the barn.

Chapter Eighteen

Two days after Marina left Cowboy Creek, Jane packed her bags for her own departure.

When she and her family had all finished breakfast, Jed called her into his den, where he made his unhappiness at her decision very clear.

"No need to go rushing off, is there? With everyone else leaving after the wedding, things have quieted down a mite too much for me."

She forced a laugh. "You've still got lots of people around here to keep you company. And Tina says she has reservations on the books for the rest of the summer. That will keep you busy."

"She'll be busier still with all the guests around, too. It's a big job for her, trying to juggle the contractors and the renovations, along with her regular bookkeeping. She could use some help."

"Andi's planning to come back soon."

"Yes, so she said, and the more the merrier, I say. We can use all the hands we can get around here. We've still got a ways to go before we'll be ready to get the wedding business up and running."

"And Tina's right on schedule with her timetable."

"You always were a darned argumentative child." He gave an unconvincingly irritated scowl, followed immediately by a sigh. "Well, what about your part in all this? It doesn't matter where you are if you're putting together the website on the computer. You said that yourself."

"I did."

"Then here would work just as well as anywhere else."

"But it wouldn't. I can't stay, Grandpa. I've already got other work lined up."

Like Marina, she had an enticing new assignment awaiting her, one that would take her from New York to Geneva, with a few stops for interviews and photos in between. If only that could be far enough from Garland Ranch to make her forget what she was leaving behind.

In the past two days, her path hadn't crossed with Pete's again.

Cole said Pete had spent those days out on the ranch on horseback, communicating with the other men mostly by cell phone. And that he had headed home earlier in the evening than usual.

As Rachel hadn't been near the Hitching Post, they all had to assume he was keeping her close to home, too.

Tina had followed through on her plan, calling Sharon about having Rachel come to play with Robbie. She hadn't gotten anywhere with that.

If anyone would know what was going on with Pete and his kids, it would be Jed. But for the past couple of days, he had been quiet, almost brooding. She suspected Pete's situation upset him even more than it did everyone else on the ranch.

They all cared about Pete and his family, yet no one knew how to help.

A hundred times, Jane considered and then rejected the idea of simply walking over to his house and knocking on the door. But as much as she wanted to see Rachel and Eric...and Pete...she wouldn't go against his wishes.

Wishes he had turned into an order harsher than any her dad had ever given her.

She rose and walked around behind Jed's desk to give him a hug. "Thanks for wanting to have me around, Grandpa," she said softly. "I really wish I could tell you I'll stay." The sudden tightness in her chest underscored the truth of that.

"I haven't given up on you yet," he said.

She shook her head, but kept silent. She couldn't tell him the true reason it was time to go home.

AFTER A QUIET family lunch, only Jane and Tina remained in the dining room. Upstairs, her bag sat packed, ready for her trip to the airport. Ready to go home.

"I'm going to miss you," Tina said. "So are Robbie and Cole and Abuela. I don't think I need to mention how sorry Grandpa is to see you go."

"Are you trying to make me feel better, coz?"

"I'm hoping to get you to change your mind."

Jane fiddled with the cutlery on her empty plate. "I told you before, I can't."

"Can't or don't want to?" Tina sighed. "You're sure there's nothing you can say to Pete, nothing you can do? Or any way I can help you?"

She shook her head. "No, but thanks. I appreciate the offer. Listening to me vent for a while was help enough."

They sat quietly for another moment.

The sound of running footsteps in the hallway suddenly made her throat tighten. How funny—she knew it wasn't Robbie's sneakers hitting the floor, but Rachel's. She hadn't seen the little girl for a couple of days now, and she had missed Rachel's enthusiastic chatter almost as much as she'd missed Pete.

Wide-eyed, Rachel skidded to a stop in the doorway.

"Jane! Paz told me you're leaving!" She ran to Jane and threw her arms around her waist.

As Jane hugged her, Tina stood and slipped from the room.

Rachel leaned back in her arms and looked up. "Are you leaving, Jane? Is that really, really true?"

She wouldn't lie to Pete's daughter. She would not make empty promises. But, unable to answer, all she could do was nod.

Rachel's shoulders slumped, and her eyes misted. A plump tear ran down her flushed cheek. She gulped once. Then nodded. "That's okay, Jane," she said quietly. "Everybody leaves me."

Jane bit her lip to hold back a sob.

She held Rachel to her, tucking the little girl's head beneath her chin, protecting her from seeing the tears filling her own eyes.

"PETE."

Startled, he looked up from his paperwork.

Jed had managed to enter the barn and come all the way to the office doorway without him noticing. Just one more indication of how his focus had been shot to pieces since he'd taken his frustration out on Jane.

In the couple of days since that afternoon with her outside the corral, he hadn't encountered her again. He hadn't seen the boss. He hadn't spoken much to anyone, except his kids and Sharon.

"Hey, Jed." He stood and gestured to the paperwork spread on the desk. "I've been gathering info on the new irrigation system. Have a seat, if you want to take a look."

"Some other time."

Jed settled on the wooden stool near the office wall and, as far as Pete could tell, stared at nothing. Above

Jed's white eyebrows, frown lines Pete had never seen before scored the old man's forehead. Plainly, Jed was worried. He also seemed to be having as much trouble concentrating as he himself had lately.

"Something up, boss?"

"Jane's gone."

Pete froze, both at the memory of her telling him exactly that about Marina and at the feeling he'd just been kicked somewhere near his heart.

Hell, after the way he'd blown up, what had he expected? That Jane would sit around hoping he would calm down? Her hair would turn white as Jed's before that would happen.

Even if he could get over what she'd done, he still would have the same reasons he'd always had for keeping his distance from her. One long, sweet night and a short but steamy meeting in a honeymoon cabin couldn't change that.

"Well..." He forced a casual shrug. "The day of the wedding, she said she had to get back to tackle a full schedule."

A schedule that would keep her busy for the next three years.

Maybe by then his anger would have subsided. But he doubted it. Her interference had affected his family more than she could ever know, and he would be dealing with the aftermath well into his future.

"I tried my darnedest to get her to stay, and she wouldn't," Jed said. "Stubborn girl. Always was, always will be. Sometimes a man's own family—and friends—can't see what's good for them. Not even when they've got someone standing right there to show them the way."

Obviously, the boss wanted to help his ranch manager and his granddaughter find their way.

That night at the Cantina, Cole had definitely gotten it right about Jed's matchmaking plans. But Pete had gotten it right, too. The boss was doomed to disappointment.

"I get what you're saying, Jed. Believe me, I do. And you can try to show people all you want. But you know as well as I do, sometimes family and friends need to figure things out for themselves."

He'd figured Jane out, all right, and didn't like his conclusions. Just like Marina, she would never choose family over career. And just like Marina, she wasn't to be trusted with his kids…or his heart.

OUTSIDE HER APARTMENT BUILDING, Jane hailed a cab and climbed into it with half her usual amount of energy.

Her driver made eye contact in the rearview mirror. Judging by the name on his operator's license, he was of Russian and Irish descent. His radio played scratchy reggae music. He had pinned a Republican campaign button to one visor, and to the other he had plastered a sticker reading "Go Democrat or Go Home."

She loved New York.

"Where we going today, lady?" His accent was pure South Bronx.

"LaGuardia," she said, then sat back for the ride to the airport.

He pulled the taxi into traffic. Apparently oblivious to the car horns protesting behind them, he said, "So, what's next on the itinerary once you take off outta there?"

"Oslo."

"That up in Canada?"

"No, it's in Norway."

"Good deal. Get you away from this muck for a while."

He meant the weather. July in the city was hot and

sticky, and for days now, the air had hazed with a blend of humidity and smog.

She loved Manhattan at any time of the year, and normally, the summer weather didn't affect her. But many things that normally didn't bother her seemed to upset her lately.

The humidity. The press of the crowds on the sidewalks. The stale air forced through sidewalk gratings by the rushing subway trains below. The rising price of her daily morning cup of tea from the Korean deli on her street corner.

"You headed off on a nice, long vacation?" the driver asked.

The thought of a break sounded tempting. Even her recent assignments, so enticing when she had first accepted them, had turned out to be as stale as the subway air. "No, it's a business trip, just till the end of the week."

"Long way to go for such a short time."

"It is, isn't it?"

By comparison, her arrival home from Cowboy Creek was a lifetime away. In these two long weeks, nothing had held her interest, not the call from Pete's father with the name of an interested gallery owner in Santa Fe or even the portfolio she had started and then set aside.

"Travel a lot, do you?" the driver asked.

"Yes. I'm usually on the road a couple of weeks out of the month."

"I'm on the road every *day*," he said with a laugh, "only you don't see me going places like Oslo."

"There are a lot of good points about staying at home, too."

"If you say so."

Funny. She had so looked forward to escaping small-town Cowboy Creek and returning home to her own world. Why didn't it seem like the same world that had once thrilled her?

"You must not have a family, huh? Or else you probably couldn't travel so much."

The man should add *clairvoyant* to his operator's license. Every topic he raised was one she had thought about over and over again during the past two weeks.

"I do have a family. None of my relatives are close by, though."

"Aww. Now, that's bad. I'll betcha you miss them."

"I do."

She missed Jed. She missed Tina and Cole and Robbie. Rachel and Eric, too. Most of all, she missed Pete.

Those unsuspected motherly instincts she had discovered had somehow given her the key to understanding his feelings about his kids.

Other instincts made her lonely and frustrated without him.

"All those frequent-flier miles," the driver said suddenly. "You can go visit soon!"

No, she couldn't. But he'd sounded so happy to have come up with the idea, she didn't have the heart to disagree.

Instead, she asked, "What's with the campaign button and the sticker? They're contradictory, aren't they?"

"Maybe so. But, see, I got talking with a fare one day. Not on politics—that's a loaded topic you don't wanna get into in a closed space like this one." He laughed again. "But just on life in general, y'know? People. Their differences. Their dreams.

"Well, anyhow, I put those things up on the visors. They do a good job reminding me everybody's story's got two sides."

Just like the stories she helped to tell.

Why couldn't Pete keep such an open mind?

JED SAT ON the front porch swing and watched the sun plummet toward the horizon. It about matched his mood. With two of his three granddaughters gone home, his progress had come to a halt. Not on the renovations—Tina was keeping up on those—but on the plan to get his granddaughters wed.

He had to think of something. He tapped a large brown envelope on his knee and contemplated his next move. His reputation as a matchmaker was on the line, even if only a handful of people knew what he was up to. And it was more than reputation that drove him—it was the need to see his family settled.

Paz stepped out onto the porch. She was still drying her hands on her apron. "What are you doing out here all by yourself?"

"I don't rightly know." He sighed. "Here, I thought I'd made some headway with Jane. Instead, the girl has abandoned us."

"She had to go back to her job."

He didn't know if the sympathy in her tone was meant for him or Jane. "Well, she's left me up a creek."

Over near Pete's, a car pulled into the driveway, one he recognized at a glance. Mark Brannigan's.

Pete's daughter climbed from the car and trudged up the steps.

"Rachel has been moping since Jane left," Paz said.

"Yeah, the poor kid. But that's nothing compared to the long face on her daddy. And *my* hands are tied."

"No, they're not. They're full."

"So they are." He looked down at the envelope he'd retrieved from the postbox at the end of the drive and had forgotten he still held. Then he looked up at Paz and smiled. “I think this packet had better get to where it’s intended to go. Don’t you?”

She nodded.

“And I think while Mark’s over at Pete’s, I ought to have a talk with him.”

“That also sounds like a good idea.”

They watched Mark lift Eric from his carrier. As he walked toward the steps with the boy, Jed rose from his seat.

If he couldn’t get at one half of the perfect pair, he’d have to work on the one he had available. Everything would all come out right at the end. He was sure of it.

Meanwhile, he’d hedge his bets.

Waving the envelope, he hailed the other man.

Chapter Nineteen

As Pete made his way home from the barn, he saw his father leaning against one fender of his luxury car, parked in front of the house. Just what he didn't need.

He didn't know what the heck he *did* need.

Jane had been gone for a couple of weeks now. With Rachel's moodiness, Eric's increased crankiness and even Sharon's tendency to withdraw into herself, proof of her worry over him and the kids, he hadn't been having a good life.

The hollowness in the pit of his stomach spread upward. He didn't want to think about what he was feeling…or what he was missing.

When he reached the house, his dad nodded to him. "I'm on the run again. I took the kids for ice cream while I waited for you. I had a long talk with Jed, too. He asked me to give you this." He held out a bulky brown envelope.

Pete shoved it under his arm. "My walking papers?"

Mark smiled. "I don't think so. In fact, the man speaks very highly of you. He always has. He knows you well, too, probably better than I do."

"Dad. Let's not get into it right now."

"I didn't plan to. But I have to tell you, though I'm a damned good interrogator, I pale by comparison to Jed."

Despite his mood, Pete laughed. "He's a hard man to beat at anything."

"I noticed. He was telling me how successfully he'd gotten Tina and Cole together. He also told me he was holding out hope for you."

He stilled and looked out over the ranch toward the barn, the Hitching Post and a corner of the small cabin where he'd spent two of the best times of his life. "*Was* is the key word. I'm not in the market for a romance."

"She's a good woman."

Startled, he turned back to stare at his father.

"Don't think I didn't notice something between you and Jane that night I was here for dinner."

"There wasn't anything." He couldn't let it go at that. Sighing, he added, "Even if there had been, that's over now. I'm happy being out of touch here on the ranch."

"As to that…you know, your mother would have been very happy to see how you've turned out. She'd be especially pleased about Rachel and Eric."

It was probably the closest his dad would ever come to an acceptance of what he wanted to do with his life. And, after a moment's thought, he decided it was near enough.

He reached out, and they shook hands.

He stood watching until the car disappeared down the road. Then he looked down at the envelope Jed had sent. An envelope with his name on it, a New York postmark and no return address.

Taking a seat on the top porch step, he opened the envelope. Inside was a large packet of photos, which he flipped through one by one. Rachel and Eric and Sharon smiled up at him. Jed and each and every member of his family did, too. Sugar and Layne and her son were there, as well as the entire wedding party. She'd even included a photo of Daffodil.

The only face he didn't find in the whole danged packet was the one belonging to…the person who had sent it. She hadn't included a single photo of herself. She had given him nothing to remember her by but memories.

The door opened behind him, and a moment later Rachel sat beside him. "What's that, Daddy?"

Her listless tone hurt his heart. "Pictures," he said. She leaned against him as, again, he flipped through them one by one. "See, there's you in your pretty dress for the wedding. And one of you with Miss Loring at your graduation. And here's one with you and me and Eric."

"Uh-huh." She'd barely glanced at the photos. "I miss Jane, Daddy."

Not Mama. *Jane.*

"I…" He had to swallow hard past the lump in his throat. "I know you do, sweetheart."

"I love Jane."

He wrapped his arm around her and kissed the top of her head. He couldn't raise false hopes or make empty promises. Instead, he said nothing.

There *was* nothing he could add, except *I love Jane, too.*

PETE REINED IN and dismounted in front of the barn.

He'd put in a long day on the ranch again, just one of a series of long, lonely days. For a man who wanted to keep himself to himself, he was surprised to find this self-inflicted routine getting old.

Well, the work on the ranch needed to be done. He didn't shirk his duties, hadn't avoided his men. Wasn't trying to head off alone to nurse his wounds—not like the days after he'd made his break from Jane. Now he was just grabbing every chance he could to keep working on his own.

Solitary confinement—though he wasn't confined at all on the open land of Garland Ranch. Maybe better said, solitary punishment for the guilt he felt every time he thought about Jane.

For the chance he hadn't grabbed when he'd had the opportunity.

Instead, he had blamed her, bitterly and to her face, for bringing his ex in contact with his kids.

In the short time she had been on the ranch, hadn't Jane been better than their own mother to his kids…and *for* his kids? She had defended his daughter and captivated his son. She had made Rachel feel special.

She had tried to get her point across to him, and he had refused to listen. She had made plenty of efforts to draw him out, and he had pushed her away. She had turned him inside out and stomped on his heart, and he had no one to blame but himself.

"Hey, Pete!"

He looked across the yard to find Jed loping toward him, an ear-to-ear grin spread across his face.

He smiled in return. He could use something to lighten his maudlin mood, and judging by the boss's expression, he would soon learn something that would take care of that. "What's up? You look fit to bust."

"That's because I am. Tina just passed along some news from both Andi and Jane."

His mood threatened to weigh him down again. "Yeah? Must be good news, from the way you're acting."

"Nope. Not good. Great. We've booked the first guest wedding for the banquet hall next month, thanks to Andi. She's headed back here as we speak, since we're looking at such a tight deadline. And Jane's coming home to help Tina and Andi pull things together."

"That *is* great news. I'm glad the business is starting to move."

He was glad for himself, too, for the chance to see Jane again. Hell, he was downright ecstatic…until reality hit.

He'd accused Jane of being just like his ex. Of putting her career ahead of her family. Of caring about no one but herself. He'd misjudged her, refused to respond to her, ordered her to stay away.

She wouldn't come near him again. After that, why would she?

This trip back to the ranch might be just as fleeting as Jane's first one. That meant he still couldn't risk her getting close to Rachel and Eric.

Regardless, he'd need to see her.

He would probably never get her to forgive him, and he would live with that. But he couldn't live with himself if he didn't give her the apology she deserved.

"YOU'VE COME a long way since I've been gone," Jane said, looking at the covered surface of the long dining room table. Contracts, employment applications, supply-house brochures and other paperwork shared the space with fabric swatches and sample wedding favors.

"Tina's got so much of the paperwork in order already," Andi said.

"And Andi's turning out to be a natural as a wedding planner," Tina said.

"Well, I guess I'm going to have to add on another job to help Grandpa reach his dream."

"Don't you worry," Jed assured her. "With this wedding coming up so soon, we'll have plenty for you to do around here."

She smiled. She would need plenty to help her stay

busy. To keep her mind occupied and away from wondering what was going to happen when she spoke with Pete.

If she spoke with Pete. Three weeks of separation could have given him an opportunity to cool down. On the other hand, it might only have given him time to dwell on everything she had done.

"Take a look at this, Jane."

Andi pushed a heavy book closer to her, and they bent their heads over it, studying the samples.

"With the decor in the banquet hall, this would look great in a darker teal," she said, fingering a lighter swatch of fabric.

Andi and Tina exchanged smiles.

"What?" she asked.

Andi laughed. "I told Tina you were going to be good for more than setting up the website."

"Gee, thanks, coz. I appreciate the backhanded vote of confidence."

"If you're looking for something else to work on," Jed said, "why don't we take a walk? I've got a few things I'd like to run by you."

"Sure." She closed the sample book. "Don't get too far ahead of me," she told her cousins.

She followed Jed to his den and took a seat on the leather couch that sat against one wall. "What's on your mind, Grandpa?"

"Well, first off, a few things that didn't get cleared up on your last visit."

Footsteps in the hallway, approaching the den, made her sit bolt upright on the couch.

Jed sat back in his chair and smiled. Not for one minute did she fall for his expression of innocence.

When Pete stopped in the doorway and she saw the

look on his face, she found some consolation in the fact that he hadn't expected to see her here, either.

"C'mon in," Jed said, rising. "I was just telling Jane we needed to take care of some unfinished business. That business is between the two of you. Now, I don't mean to be sticking my nose in where I'm not wanted—What's that, Pete?"

"Just a tickle in my throat, boss." The cough he hid behind his fist seemed just as contrived as Jed's smile. Or maybe it was a nervous reaction.

She frowned. "Grandpa. You set me up."

"I did not." He chuckled. "I set you both up. I've had enough of your stubbornness, girl, and enough of seeing my manager wandering around here as if he'd lost his favorite horse in a crooked poker game. I'm leaving now. You're both on your own. And I'm going to trust you'll keep the shouting to a minimum and my den in one piece."

He crossed the room, brushed past Pete and closed the door firmly on his way out.

Pete stood where he was, his hands clamped on the brim of the hat he held in front of him.

"I didn't hear Grandpa lock the door behind him," she said. "I guess that means we can leave anytime we want. But if you're staying and holding on to your cowboy hat, I should at least have my camera."

He frowned. "What for?"

"My shield, remember?"

"Do you think you'll need one?"

"I don't know. Do you need one?"

"I'm planning to let mine down." He tossed the Stetson onto a guest chair and rested back against the edge of the desk. "Where do I start?"

"With 'how are you?' But I can save you the trouble. I'm happy to be back."

"I'm happy to see you." At his smile, her heart seemed to swell. "That wasn't so much the case the last time we saw each other. I've got some apologizing to do over that, if you'll let me. And some explaining, too, if you've got the time."

"I have lots and lots of time. Why don't we start with the explanations?"

"About Rachel and the makeup. You've probably figured it out by now, but I overreacted. I realize my concerns about her wearing the makeup and wanting her picture taken are all tied up in how I feel about Marina's career."

"Rachel only likes to play dress-up in a mirror. She hasn't made a life decision about it yet. And as you said to me once, she's only five. Even if she does begin to get interested in following in her mother's footsteps, she'll probably have changed her mind twelve times before she's grown up."

"I thought you didn't know much about kids."

"Well, as *I* said once, I was one." She smiled. "And maybe I'm learning a thing or two."

"Me, too. I also figured out I'm being unfair by acting the same way about Rachel's choices—choices she hasn't even made yet—as my dad acted over mine. Just as I'm letting the way Marina treats the kids affect my beliefs about how you'll be with them, too. Only I've already seen you with them, and you're nothing like that. Nothing at all. You're good for them."

"Thank you," she murmured. "You don't know how much that means."

"You're good for me, too."

Her breath caught at his words. She loved hearing

them, wanted to believe them. Yet he'd spoken in a monotone, hadn't smiled and now couldn't meet her eyes. "Then why do you look so unhappy?"

He braced his hands on the desktop on either side of him. "Because there's not a lot I can do about it, no matter how much I care about you. And I do care. Those times in the cabin—"

"Those times we made love."

"Yes. I wouldn't have been there, making love with you, if I didn't care. No matter how I tried, I couldn't stay away. I couldn't admit this then, either, but I already loved you."

Sudden moisture made her eyes blur. But how could he talk about loving her and still look so unhappy? She clamped one hand on the arm of the couch to keep from crossing the room to him.

"I love you, Jane. I love my kids, too. They're my life. And I can't knowingly put them through what happened when Marina first left."

"I realize how hard it must have been—"

"No," he said heavily, "you don't. I've never told you the worst of it. Never told anyone. Only Sharon knows the truth, and only because she was there to witness it." He ran his hand through his hair and stared at the closed door. "When Marina walked out, Eric stopped sleeping, stopped taking his bottle, cried for hours on end. Colic, some doctors said. Milk allergies, other doctors said. And maybe those were the answers. I don't know."

He looked down at the floor.

Quickly, she brushed at her eyes.

When he spoke again, his voice was low and rough and unsteady. "All I do know is, whenever I held Eric to feed him, I would offer him his bottle and he'd turn his head away. He didn't want what I was trying to give him.

He wanted what he knew. Not formula, but his mother's milk. And his mother wasn't there anymore."

Her breath caught. She raised her hand to her mouth, holding back a sob.

When he looked up at her again, unshed tears filled his eyes.

She stood, wanting to go to him, but he held up his hand. Not in anger the way he had weeks ago, she could see that, but because he was fighting for control.

"Rachel went back to sucking her thumb and wetting the bed at night." He shook his head. "I was watching my daughter become a baby again and my son nearly waste away. All because their mama put her career above them."

Tears flowed down her cheeks now, and she couldn't stay away. She crossed the room to him, pressed her forehead against his shoulder, felt his arms go around her. He was the one reliving the memories, yet he was comforting her.

Or maybe he just needed someone to hang on to.

She wrapped her arms around him and held on tight.

How long they stood together like that, Pete couldn't say. His heart had broken at seeing Jane's compassion, at knowing how he felt about her. At realizing what he had to do.

He lifted her chin, rested his fingers against her soft cheek and looked into her tear-swollen eyes.

"I love you," she said, her voice trembling.

"I love you. More than you'll ever know. But you see now?" He sighed.

"I understand what you went through," she said slowly. "And I see love's not worth a lot if it's not built on a solid relationship. But even if it is, there's still risk and faith involved."

"I've got the faith. I know we'd be good together. As

for risk...well, not too long ago, I was afraid to risk telling you I love you."

"It didn't go so badly today."

"No. Not at all." He stroked her cheek. "But after what my kids went through... Jane, that's one risk I can't take. I can't bring someone into their lives who isn't going to stick around. And I can't ask you to give up your career for us."

"I already have."

He froze.

"Grandpa didn't tell you?"

"Tell me what?"

"I'm on the ranch to stay. I've still got some outstanding commitments to keep, but the assignments I'll take in the future will be much different. Including the show your dad helped me line up at a gallery in Santa Fe."

"I owe that man a big thank-you."

She smiled. "I'll plan to be there when you tell him that. And I'll make sure all my future assignments are close to home. Which, from now on, is the Hitching Post Hotel."

He stared, still unable to believe what he was hearing.

She touched his face. "I love you, Pete. I can't promise you I'll be an overnight success as a mom, but I can promise you I'll try."

"That's something I *can* ask of the woman I love." He smiled. "And if you need the extra practice, we can always have a few more kids."

"I'd love that. As long as you'll be there to help."

"Sweetheart," he whispered, "there's nowhere else this cowboy wants to go."

Epilogue

Two weeks later

Jed Garland was a satisfied man.

All three of his granddaughters and every one of his great-grandkids had graced the breakfast table in his dining room that morning. Pete and Sharon and the kids had come for the meal, too, to complete the family gathering.

He and Paz sat at that table having a last cup of coffee.

At the sound of running feet approaching the dining room, they both looked toward the door.

Rachel ran into the room. "Grandpa Jed! Paz! Hurry up, please. We have to get ready for the picture."

"What picture?" Jed teased.

She rolled her eyes. "Oh, you know. The picture for my first day of school!"

"Well, then, we'd better hurry along."

"Yes. As soon as Jane takes the picture, Daddy and Jane have to drive me to school."

Paz quickly untied her apron, and the three of them went through the hotel and outside to the front porch.

At the bottom of the steps, Jane was setting up her camera on a tripod. Her assistant stood very close at hand.

"I have to go help Jane and Daddy," Rachel said. She ran down the porch steps.

For a moment, Jed and Paz stood alone at the hotel's front entrance.

"Such a wonderful day, boss," Paz said.

"That it is. You know, Paz, I'm mighty pleased at our progress. The hotel renovations are moving right along. We've lined up our first guest wedding. We've got one granddaughter hitched. And just look at this, will you." He nudged her with his elbow and tilted his head to direct her attention to the family photographer. "Seeing the way Jane's kissing on that ranch manager of ours, I'm expecting we'll hear more good news at any time."

Yep, he surely was one satisfied man.

At least, for now…

* * * * *

Grandpa Jed has one single granddaughter left!
Be sure to look for Andi's story,
the next book in Barbara White Daille's
THE HITCHING POST HOTEL *series,*
available in December 2015
wherever Harlequin books are sold.

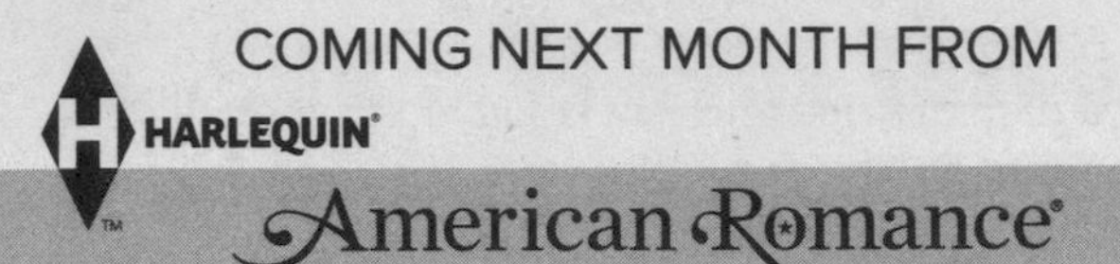

Available August 4, 2015

#1557 TEXAS REBELS: FALCON

Texas Rebels • by Linda Warren

Falcon Rebel's wife, Leah, did the unthinkable: she left him and their three-month-old baby. Now she's back, wanting to see her daughter. Will Falcon allow her into their lives again or refuse to give her a second chance?

#1558 FALLING FOR THE SHERIFF

Cupid's Bow, Texas • by Tanya Michaels

Kate Sullivan is busy raising her teenage son, and she has no interest in dating again. But single dad Cole Trent, the sheriff of Cupid's Bow, Texas, may make her change her mind!

#1559 THE TEXAS RANGER'S WIFE

Lone Star Lawmen • by Rebecca Winters

To protect herself from a dangerous stalker, champion barrel racer Kellie Parrish pretends to be married to Cy Vance, the hunky Texas Ranger assigned to her case. But it's impossible to keep their feelings about each other completely professional...

#1560 THE CONVENIENT COWBOY

by Heidi Hormel

Cowgirl Olympia James only agreed to marry her onetime fling Spence MacCormack to help him keep custody of his son. But when she discovers she's pregnant—with Spence's baby—this convenient marriage might turn into something more.

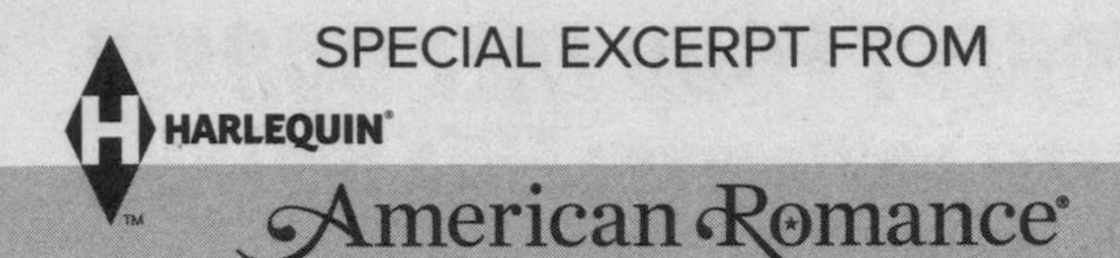

Falcon Rebel hasn't seen Leah in seventeen years...
but he's never forgotten her.

Read on for a sneak preview of
TEXAS REBELS: FALCON,
the second book in Linda Warren*'s*
exciting new series ***TEXAS REBELS.***

A truck pulled up to the curb and her thoughts came to an abrupt stop. It was Falcon.

There was no mistaking him—tall, with broad shoulders and an intimidating glare. She swallowed hard as his long strides brought him closer. In jeans, boots and a Stetson he reminded her of the first time she'd met him in high school. Being new to the school system, she was shy and didn't know a lot of the kids. It took her two years before she'd actually made friends and felt like part of a group. Falcon Rebel was way out of her group. The girls swooned over him and the boys wanted to be like him: tough and confident.

One day she was sitting on a bench waiting for her aunt to pick her up. Falcon strolled from the gym just as he was now, with broad sure strides. She never knew what made her get up from the bench, but as she did she'd dropped her books and purse and items went everywhere. He'd stopped to help her and her hands shook from the intensity of his dark eyes. From that moment on there was no one for her but Falcon.

HAREXP0715

Now he stood about twelve feet from her, and once again she felt like that shy young girl trying to make conversation. But this was so much more intense.

Be calm. Be calm. Be calm.

"I'm…I'm glad you came," she said, trying to maintain her composure because she knew the next few minutes were going to be the roughest of her life.

His eyes narrowed. "What do you want?" His words were like hard rocks hitting her skin, each one intended to import a message. His eyes were dark and angry, and she wondered if she'd made the right decision in coming here.

She gathered every ounce of courage she managed to build over the years and replied, "I want to see my daughter."

He took a step closer to her. "Does the phrase 'Over my dead body' mean anything to you?"

Don't miss TEXAS REBELS: FALCON
by Linda Warren, available August 2015
wherever Harlequin® American Romance®
books and ebooks are sold.

www.Harlequin.com

HAREXP0715

HARLEQUIN®
TM
A Romance FOR EVERY MOOD™